IN QUEST OF A
LOST IDENTITY:

Tarzan staggered to his feet and groped his way about among the underground ways of Opar. What was he? Where was he? His head ached, but otherwise he felt no ill effects from the blow that had felled him. He did not recall the accident, nor aught of what had led up to it.

At last he found the doorway leading inward beneath the city and the temple. Nothing spurred his hurt memory to a recollection of past familiarity with his surroundings. He blundered on through the darkness as though he were traversing an open plain under a noonday sun.

Suddenly he reached the brink of a well, stepped outward into space, lunged forward, and shot downward into the inky depths below. Still clutching his spear, he struck the water and sank beneath its surface . . .

The *Authorized Editions* of
Edgar Rice Burroughs'
TARZAN NOVELS
Published by Ballantine Books:

COMPLETE AND UNABRIDGED!

TARZAN AND THE JEWELS OF OPAR

Edgar Rice Burroughs

BALLANTINE BOOKS • NEW YORK

CONTENTS

1

Belgian and Arab

L IEUTENANT Albert Werper had only the prestige of the name he had dishonored to thank for his narrow escape from being cashiered. At first he had been humbly thankful, too, that they had sent him to this Godforsaken Congo post instead of court-martialing him, as he had so justly deserved; but now six months of the monotony, the frightful isolation and the loneliness had wrought a change. The young man brooded continually over his fate. His days were filled with morbid self-pity, which eventually engendered in his weak and vacillating mind a hatred for those who had sent him here—for the very men he had at first inwardly thanked for saving him from the ignominy of degradation.

He regretted the gay life of Brussels as he never had regretted the sins which had snatched him from that gayest of capitals, and as the days passed he came to center his resentment upon the representative in Congo land of the authority which had exiled him—his captain and immediate superior.

This officer was a cold, taciturn man, inspiring little love in those directly beneath him, yet respected and feared by the black soldiers of his little command.

Werper was accustomed to sit for hours glaring at his superior as the two sat upon the veranda of their common quarters, smoking their evening cigarets in a silence which neither seemed desirous of breaking. The senseless hatred of the lieutenant grew at last into a form of mania. The captain's natural taciturnity he distorted into a studied attempt to insult him because of his past shortcomings. He imagined that his superior held him in contempt, and so he chafed and fumed inwardly until one evening his madness became suddenly homicidal. He fingered the butt of the revolver at his hip, his eyes narrowed and his brows contracted. At last he spoke.

"You have insulted me for the last time!" he cried, springing to his feet. "I am an officer and a gentleman, and I shall put up with it no longer without an accounting from you, you pig."

The captain, an expression of surprise upon his features, turned toward his junior. He had seen men before with the jungle madness upon them—the madness of solitude and unrestrained brooding, and perhaps a touch of fever.

He rose and extended his hand to lay it upon the other's shoulder. Quiet words of counsel were upon his lips; but they were never spoken. Werper construed his superior's action into an attempt to close with him. His revolver was on a level with the captain's heart, and the latter had taken but a step when Werper pulled the trigger. Without a moan the man sank to the rough planking of the veranda, and as he fell the mists that had clouded Werper's brain lifted, so that he saw himself and the deed that he had done in the same light that those who must judge him would see them.

He heard excited exclamations from the quarters of the soldiers and he heard men running in his direction. They would seize him, and if they didn't kill him they would take him down the Congo to a point where a properly ordered military tribunal would do so just as effectively, though in a more regular manner.

Werper had no desire to die. Never before had he so yearned for life as in this moment that he had so effectively forfeited his right to live. The men were nearing him. What was he to do? He glanced about as though searching for the tangible form of a legitimate excuse for his crime; but he could find only the body of the man he had so causelessly shot down.

In despair, he turned and fled from the oncoming soldiery. Across the compound he ran, his revolver still clutched tightly in his hand. At the gates a sentry halted him. Werper did not pause to parley or to exert the influence of his commission—he merely raised his weapon and shot down the innocent black. A moment later the fugitive had torn open the gates and vanished into the blackness of the jungle, but not before he had transferred the rifle and ammunition belts of the dead sentry to his own person.

All that night Werper fled farther and farther into the heart of the wilderness. Now and again the voice of a lion brought him to a listening halt; but with cocked and ready rifle he pushed ahead again, more fearful of the human huntsmen in his rear than of the wild carnivora ahead.

Dawn came at last, but still the man plodded on. All sense of hunger and fatigue were lost in the terrors of contemplated capture. He could think only of escape. He dared not pause to rest or eat until there was no further danger from pursuit, and so he staggered on until at last he fell and could rise no more. How long he had fled he did not know, or try to know. When he could flee no longer the knowledge that he had reached his limit was hidden from him in the unconsciousness of utter exhaustion.

And thus it was that Achmet Zek, the Arab, found him. Achmet's followers were for running a spear through the body of their hereditary enemy; but Achmet would have it otherwise. First he would question the Belgian. It were easier to question a man first and kill him afterward, than kill him first and then question him.

So he had Lieutenant Albert Werper carried to his own tent, and there slaves administered wine and food in small quantities until at last the prisoner regained consciousness. As he opened his eyes he saw the faces of strange black men about him, and just outside the tent the figure of an Arab. Nowhere was the uniform of his soldiers to be seen.

The Arab turned and seeing the open eyes of the prisoner upon him, entered the tent.

"I am Achmet Zek," he announced. "Who are you, and what were you doing in my country? Where are your soldiers?"

Achmet Zek! Werper's eyes went wide, and his heart sank. He was in the clutches of the most notorious of cutthroats—a hater of all Europeans, especially those who wore the uniform of Belgium. For years the military forces of Belgian Congo had waged a fruitless war upon this man and his followers—a war in which quarter had never been asked nor expected by either side.

But presently in the very hatred of the man for Belgians, Werper saw a faint ray of hope for himself. He, too, was an outcast and an outlaw. So far, at least, they possessed a common interest, and Werper decided to play upon it for all that it might yield.

"I have heard of you," he replied, "and was searching for you. My people have turned against me. I hate them. Even now their soldiers are searching for me, to kill me. I knew that you would protect me from them, for you, too, hate them. In return I will take service with you. I am a trained soldier. I can fight, and your enemies are my enemies."

Achmet Zek eyed the European in silence. In his mind

he revolved many thoughts, chief among which was that
the unbeliever lied. Of course there was the chance that he
did not lie, and if he told the truth then his proposition
was one well worthy of consideration, since fighting men
were never over plentiful—especially white men with the
training and knowledge of military matters that a European
officer must possess.

Achmet Zek scowled and Werper's heart sank; but Werper
did not know Achmet Zek, who was quite apt to scowl where
another would smile, and smile where another would scowl.

"And if you have lied to me," said Achmet Zek, "I will
kill you at any time. What return, other than your life, do
you expect for your services?"

"My keep only, at first," replied Werper. "Later, if I am
worth more, we can easily reach an understanding." Werper's only desire at the moment was to preserve his life.
And so the agreement was reached and Lieutenant Albert
Werper became a member of the ivory and slave raiding
band of the notorious Achmet Zek.

For months the renegade Belgian rode with the savage
raiders. He fought with a savage abandon, and a vicious
cruelty fully equal to that of his fellow desperadoes. Achmet
Zek watched his recruit with eagle eye, and with a growing
satisfaction which finally found expression in a greater confidence in the man, and resulted in an increased indepen-
dence of action for Werper.

Achmet Zek took the Belgian into his confidence to a great
extent, and at last unfolded to him a pet scheme which the
Arab had long fostered, but which he never had found an
opportunity to effect. With the aid of a European, however,
the thing might be easily accomplished. He sounded
Werper.

"You have heard of the man men call Tarzan?" he asked.

Werper nodded. "I have heard of him; but I do not know
him."

"But for him we might carry on our 'trading' in safety
and with great profit," continued the Arab. "For years he has
fought us, driving us from the richest part of the country,
harassing us, and arming the natives that they may repel us
when we come to 'trade.' He is very rich. If we could find
some way to make him pay us many pieces of gold we
should not only be avenged upon him; but repaid for much
that he has prevented us from winning from the natives
under his protection."

Werper withdrew a cigaret from a jeweled case and
lighted it.

"And you have a plan to make him pay?" he asked.

"He has a wife," replied Achmet Zek, "whom men say is very beautiful. She would bring a great price farther north, if we found it too difficult to collect ransom money from this Tarzan."

Werper bent his head in thought. Achmet Zek stood awaiting his reply. What good remained in Albert Werper revolted at the thought of selling a white woman into the slavery and degradation of a Moslem harem. He looked up at Achmet Zek. He saw the Arab's eyes narrow, and he guessed that the other had sensed his antagonism to the plan. What would it mean to Werper to refuse? His life lay in the hands of this semi-barbarian, who esteemed the life of an unbeliever less highly than that of a dog. Werper loved life. What was this woman to him, anyway? She was a European, doubtless, a member of organized society. He was an outcast. The hand of every white man was against him. She was his natural enemy, and if he refused to lend himself to her undoing, Achmet Zek would have him killed.

"You hesitate," murmured the Arab.

"I was but weighing the chances of success," lied Werper, "and my reward. As a European I can gain admittance to their home and table. You have no other with you who could do so much. The risk will be great. I should be well paid, Achmet Zek."

A smile of relief passed over the raider's face.

"Well said, Werper," and Achmet Zek slapped his lieutenant upon the shoulder. "You should be well paid and you shall. Now let us sit together and plan how best the thing may be done," and the two men squatted upon a soft rug beneath the faded silks of Achmet's once gorgeous tent, and talked together in low voices well into the night. Both were tall and bearded, and the exposure to sun and wind had given an almost Arab hue to the European's complexion. In every detail of dress, too, he copied the fashions of his chief, so that outwardly he was as much an Arab as the other. It was late when he arose and retired to his own tent.

The following day Werper spent in overhauling his Belgian uniform, removing from it every vestige of evidence that might indicate its military purposes. From a heterogeneous collection of loot, Achmet Zek procured a pith helmet and a European saddle, and from his black slaves and followers a party of porters, askaris and tent boys to make up a modest safari for a big game hunter. At the head of this party Werper set out from camp.

2

On the Road To Opar

IT WAS two weeks later that John Clayton, Lord Greystoke, riding in from a tour of inspection of his vast African estate, glimpsed the head of a column of men crossing the plain that lay between his bungalow and the forest to the north and west.

He reined in his horse and watched the little party as it emerged from a concealing swale. His keen eyes caught the reflection of the sun upon the white helmet of a mounted man, and with the conviction that a wandering European hunter was seeking his hospitality, he wheeled his mount and rode slowly forward to meet the newcomer.

A half hour later he was mounting the steps leading to the veranda of his bungalow, and introducing M. Jules Frecoult to Lady Greystoke.

"I was completely lost," M. Frecoult was explaining. "My head man had never before been in this part of the country and the guides who were to have accompanied me from the last village we passed knew even less of the country than we. They finally deserted us two days since. I am very fortunate indeed to have stumbled so providentially upon succor. I do not know what I should have done, had I not found you."

It was decided that Frecoult and his party should remain several days, or until they were thoroughly rested, when Lord Greystoke would furnish guides to lead them safely back into country with which Frecoult's head man was supposedly familiar.

In his guise of a French gentleman of leisure, Werper found little difficulty in deceiving his host and in ingratiating himself with both Tarzan and Jane Clayton; but the longer he remained the less hopeful he became of an easy accomplishment of his designs.

Lady Greystoke never rode alone at any great distance from the bungalow, and the savage loyalty of the ferocious Waziri warriors who formed a great part of Tarzan's followers seemed to preclude the possibility of a successful attempt at forcible abduction, or of the bribery of the Waziri themselves.

A week passed, and Werper was no nearer the fulfillment of his plan, in so far as he could judge, than upon the day of his arrival, but at that very moment something occurred which gave him renewed hope and set his mind upon an even greater reward than a woman's ransom.

A runner had arrived at the bungalow with the weekly mail, and Lord Greystoke had spent the afternoon in his study reading and answering letters. At dinner he seemed distraught, and early in the evening he excused himself and retired, Lady Greystoke following him very soon after. Werper, sitting upon the veranda, could hear their voices in earnest discussion, and having realized that something of unusual moment was afoot, he quietly rose from his chair, and keeping well in the shadow of the shrubbery growing profusely about the bungalow, made his silent way to a point beneath the window of the room in which his host and hostess slept.

Here he listened, and not without result, for almost the first words he overheard filled him with excitement. Lady Greystoke was speaking as Werper came within hearing.

"I always feared for the stability of the company," she was saying; "but it seems incredible that they should have failed for so enormous a sum—unless there has been some dishonest manipulation."

"That is what I suspect," replied Tarzan; "but whatever the cause, the fact remains that I have lost everything, and there is nothing for it but to return to Opar and get more."

"Oh, John," cried Lady Greystoke, and Werper could feel the shudder through her voice, "is there no other way? I cannot bear to think of you returning to that frightful city. I would rather live in poverty always than to have you risk the hideous dangers of Opar."

"You need have no fear," replied Tarzan, laughing. "I am pretty well able to take care of myself, and were I not, the Waziri who will accompany me will see that no harm befalls me."

"They ran away from Opar once, and left you to your fate," she reminded him.

"They will not do it again," he answered. "They were very much ashamed of themselves, and were coming back when I met them."

"But there must be some other way," insisted the woman.

"There is no other way half so easy to obtain another fortune, as to go to the treasure vaults of Opar and bring it away," he replied. "I shall be very careful, Jane, and the chances are that the inhabitants of Opar will never know that

I have been there again and despoiled them of another portion of the treasure, the very existence of which they are as ignorant of as they would be of its value."

The finality in his tone seemed to assure Lady Greystoke that further argument was futile, and so she abandoned the subject.

Werper remained, listening, for a short time, and then, confident that he had overheard all that was necessary and fearing discovery, returned to the veranda, where he smoked numerous cigarets in rapid succession before retiring.

The following morning at breakfast, Werper announced his intention of making an early departure, and asked Tarzan's permission to hunt big game in the Waziri country on his way out—permission which Lord Greystoke readily granted.

The Belgian consumed two days in completing his preparations, but finally got away with his safari, accompanied by a single Waziri guide whom Lord Greystoke had loaned him. The party made but a single short march when Werper simulated illness, and announced his intention of remaining where he was until he had fully recovered. As they had gone but a short distance from the Greystoke bungalow, Werper dismissed the Waziri guide, telling the warrior that he would send for him when he was able to proceed. The Waziri gone, the Belgian summoned one of Achmet Zek's trusted blacks to his tent, and dispatched him to watch for the departure of Tarzan, returning immediately to advise Werper of the event and the direction taken by the Englishman.

The Belgian did not have long to wait, for the following day his emissary returned with word that Tarzan and a party of fifty Waziri warriors had set out toward the southeast early in the morning.

Werper called his head man to him, after writing a long letter to Achmet Zek. This letter he handed to the head man.

"Send a runner at once to Achmet Zek with this," he instructed the head man. "Remain here in camp awaiting further instructions from him or from me. If any come from the bungalow of the Englishman, tell them that I am very ill within my tent and can see no one. Now, give me six porters and six askaris—the strongest and bravest of the safari—and I will march after the Englishman and discover where his gold is hidden."

And so it was that as Tarzan, stripped to the loin cloth and armed after the primitive fashion he best loved, led his loyal Waziri toward the dead city of Opar, Werper, the renegade, haunted his trail through the long, hot days, and camped close behind him by night.

And as they marched, Achmet Zek rode with his entire following southward toward the Greystoke farm.

To Tarzan of the Apes the expedition was in the nature of a holiday outing. His civilization was at best but an outward veneer which he gladly peeled off with his uncomfortable European clothes whenever any reasonable pretext presented itself. It was a woman's love which kept Tarzan even to the semblance of civilization—a condition for which familiarity had bred contempt. He hated the shams and the hypocrisies of it and with the clear vision of an unspoiled mind he had penetrated to the rotten core of the heart of the thing—the cowardly greed for peace and ease and the safeguarding of property rights. That the fine things of life —art, music and literature—had thriven upon such enervating ideals he strenuously denied, insisting, rather, that they had endured in spite of civilization.

"Show me the fat, opulent coward," he was wont to say, "who ever originated a beautiful ideal. In the clash of arms, in the battle for survival, amid hunger and death and danger, in the face of God as manifested in the display of Nature's most terrific forces, is born all that is finest and best in the human heart and mind."

And so Tarzan always came back to Nature in the spirit of a lover keeping a long deferred tryst after a period behind prison walls. His Waziri, at marrow, were more civilized than he. They cooked their meat before they ate it and they shunned many articles of food as unclean that Tarzan had eaten with gusto all his life and so insidious is the virus of hypocrisy that even the stalwart ape-man hesitated to give rein to his natural longings before them. He ate burnt flesh when he would have preferred it raw and unspoiled, and he brought down game with arrow or spear when he would far rather have leaped upon it from ambush and sunk his strong teeth in its jugular; but at last the call of the milk of the savage mother that had suckled him in infancy rose to an insistent demand—he craved the hot blood of a fresh kill and his muscles yearned to pit themselves against the savage jungle in the battle for existence that had been his sole birthright for the first twenty years of his life.

3

The Call of the Jungle

Moved by these vague yet all-powerful urgings the ape-man lay awake one night in the little thorn boma that protected, in a way, his party from the depredations of the great carnivora of the jungle. A single warrior stood sleepy guard beside the fire that yellow eyes out of the darkness beyond the camp made imperative. The moans and the coughing of the big cats mingled with the myriad noises of the lesser denizens of the jungle to fan the savage flame in the breast of this savage English lord. He tossed upon his bed of grasses, sleepless, for an hour and then he rose, noiseless as a wraith, and while the Waziri's back was turned, vaulted the boma wall in the face of the flaming eyes, swung silently into a great tree and was gone.

For a time in sheer exuberance of animal spirit he raced swiftly through the middle terrace, swinging perilously across wide spans from one jungle giant to the next, and then he clambered upward to the swaying, lesser boughs of the upper terrace where the moon shone full upon him and the air was stirred by little breezes and death lurked ready in each frail branch. Here he paused and raised his face to Goro, the moon. With uplifted arm he stood, the cry of the bull ape quivering upon his lips, yet he remained silent lest he arouse his faithful Waziri who were all too familiar with the hideous challenge of their master.

And then he went on more slowly and with greater stealth and caution, for now Tarzan of the Apes was seeking a kill. Down to the ground he came in the utter blackness of the close-set boles and the overhanging verdure of the jungle. He stooped from time to time and put his nose close to earth. He sought and found a wide game trail and at last his nostrils were rewarded with the scent of the fresh spoor of Bara, the deer. Tarzan's mouth watered and a low growl escaped his patrician lips. Sloughed from him was the last vestige of artificial caste—once again he was the primeval hunter—the first man—the highest caste type of the human race. Up wind he followed the elusive spoor with sense of perception so transcending that of ordinary man as to be inconceivable to us. Through counter currents of the heavy stench of meat eaters he traced the trail of Bara; the sweet and cloying stink of Horta, the boar, could not drown his quarry's scent—the permeating, mellow musk of the deer's foot.

Presently the body scent of the deer told Tarzan that his prey was close at hand. It sent him into the trees again— into the lower terrace where he could watch the ground below and catch with ears and nose the first intimation of actual contact with his quarry. Nor was it long before the ape-man came upon Bara standing alert at the edge of a moon-bathed clearing. Noiselessly Tarzan crept through the trees until he was directly over the deer. In the ape-man's right hand was the long hunting knife of his father and in his heart the blood lust of the carnivore. Just for an instant he poised above the unsuspecting Bara and then he launched himself downward upon the sleek back. The impact of his weight carried the deer to its knees and before the animal could regain its feet the knife had found its heart. As Tarzan rose upon the body of his kill to scream forth his hideous victory cry into the face of the moon the wind carried to his nostrils something which froze him to statuesque immobility and silence. His savage eyes blazed into the direction from which the wind had borne down the warning to him and a moment later the grasses at one side of the clearing parted and Numa, the lion, strode majestically into view. His yellow-green eyes were fastened upon Tarzan as he halted just within the clearing and glared enviously at the successful hunter, for Numa had had no luck this night.

From the lips of the ape-man broke a rumbling growl of warning. Numa answered but he did not advance. Instead he stood waving his tail gently to and fro, and presently Tarzan squatted upon his kill and cut a generous portion from a hind quarter. Numa eyed him with growing resentment and rage as, between mouthfuls, the ape-man growled out his savage warnings. Now this particular lion had never before come in contact with Tarzan of the Apes and he was much mystified. Here was the appearance and the scent of a man-thing and Numa had tasted of human flesh and learned that though not the most palatable it was certainly by far the easiest to secure, yet there was that in the bestial growls of the strange creature which reminded him of formidable antagonists and gave him pause, while his hunger and the odor of the hot flesh of Bara goaded him almost to madness. Always Tarzan watched him, guessing what was passing in the little brain of the carnivore and well it was that he did watch him, for at last Numa could stand it no longer. His tail shot suddenly erect and at the same instant the wary ape-man, knowing all too well what the signal portended, grasped the remainder of the deer's hind quarter between his teeth and leaped into a nearby tree as Numa charged him with all the speed and a sufficient semblance of the weight of an express train.

Tarzan's retreat was no indication that he felt fear. Jungle life is ordered along different lines than ours and different standards prevail. Had Tarzan been famished he would, doubtless, have stood his ground and met the lion's charge. He had done the thing before upon more than one occasion, just as in the past he had charged lions himself; but to-night he was far from famished and in the hind quarter he had carried off with him was more raw flesh than he could eat; yet it was with no equanimity that he looked down upon Numa rending the flesh of Tarzan's kill. The presumption of this strange Numa must be punished! And forthwith Tarzan set out to make life miserable for the big cat. Close by were many trees bearing large, hard fruits and to one of these the ape-man swung with the agility of a squirrel. Then commenced a bombardment which brought forth earth-shaking roars from Numa. One after another as rapidly as he could gather and hurl them Tarzan pelted the hard fruit down upon the lion. It was impossible for the tawny cat to eat under that hail of missiles—he could but roar and growl and dodge and eventually he was driven away entirely from the carcass of Bara, the deer. He went roaring and resentful; but in the very center of the clearing his voice was suddenly hushed and Tarzan saw the great head lower and flatten out, the body crouch and the long tail quiver, as the beast slunk cautiously toward the trees upon the opposite side.

Immediately Tarzan was alert. He lifted his head and sniffed the slow, jungle breeze. What was it that had attracted Numa's attention and taken him soft-footed and silent away from the scene of his discomfiture? Just as the lion disappeared among the trees beyond the clearing Tarzan caught upon the down-coming wind the explanation of his new interest—the scent spoor of man was wafted strongly to the sensitive nostrils. Caching the remainder of the deer's hind quarter in the crotch of a tree the ape-man wiped his greasy palms upon his naked thighs and swung off in pursuit of Numa. A broad, well-beaten elephant path led into the forest from the clearing. Parallel to this slunk Numa, while above him Tarzan moved through the trees, the shadow of a wraith. The savage cat and the savage man saw Numa's quarry almost simultaneously, though both had known before it came within the vision of their eyes that it was a black man. Their sensitive nostrils had told them this much and Tarzan's had told him that the scent spoor was that of a stranger—old and a male, for race and sex and age each has its own distinctive scent. It was an old man that made his way alone through the gloomy jungle, a wrinkled, dried up, little old man hideously scarred and tattooed and strangely garbed, with the skin of a hyena about his shoulders and the dried head mounted upon his grey pate. Tarzan recognized the ear-marks of the witch-doctor and awaited Numa's charge with a feeling of pleasurable anticipation, for the ape-man had no love for witch-doctors; but in the instant that Numa did charge, the white man suddenly recalled that the lion had stolen his kill a few minutes before and that revenge is sweet.

The first intimation the black man had that he was in danger was the crash of twigs as Numa charged through the bushes into the game trail not twenty yards behind him. Then he turned to see a huge, black-maned lion racing toward him and even as he turned, Numa seized him. At the same instant the ape-man dropped from an overhanging limb full upon the lion's back and as he alighted he plunged his knife into the tawny side behind the left shoulder, tangled the fingers of his right hand in the long mane, buried his teeth in Numa's neck and wound his powerful legs about the beast's torso. With a roar of pain and rage, Numa reared up and fell backward upon the ape-man; but still the mighty man-thing clung to his hold and repeatedly the long knife plunged rapidly into his side. Over and over rolled Numa, the lion, clawing and biting at the air, roaring and growling horribly in savage attempt to reach the thing upon its back. More than once was Tarzan almost brushed from his hold. He was battered and bruised and covered with blood from Numa and dirt from the trail, yet not for an instant did he lessen the ferocity of his mad attack nor his grim hold upon the back of his antagonist. To have loosened for an instant his grip there, would have been to bring him within reach of those tearing talons or rending fangs, and have ended forever the grim career of this jungle-bred English lord. Where he had fallen beneath the spring of the lion the witch-doctor lay, torn and bleeding, unable to drag himself away and watched the terrific battle between these two lords of the jungle. His sunken eyes glittered and his wrinkled lips moved over toothless gums as he mumbled weird incantations to the demons of his cult.

For a time he felt no doubt as to the outcome—the strange white man must certainly succumb to terrible Simba

—whoever heard of a lone man armed only with a knife slaying so mighty a beast! Yet presently the old black man's eyes went wider and he commenced to have his doubts and misgivings. What wonderful sort of creature was this that battled with Simba and held his own despite the mighty muscles of the king of beasts and slowly there dawned in those sunken eyes, gleaming so brightly from the scarred and winkled face, the light of a dawning recollection. Gropingly backward into the past reached the fingers of memory, until at last they seized upon a faint picture, faded and yellow with the passing years. It was the picture of a lithe, white-skinned youth swinging through the trees in company with a band of huge apes, and the old eyes blinked and a great fear came into them—the superstitious fear of one who believes in ghosts and spirits and demons.

And came the time once more when the witch-doctor no longer doubted the outcome of the duel, yet his first judgment was reversed, for now he knew that the jungle god would slay Simba and the old black was even more terrified of his own impending fate at the hands of the victor than he had been by the sure and sudden death which the triumphant lion would have meted out to him. He saw the lion weaken from loss of blood. He saw the mighty limbs tremble and stagger and at last he saw the beast sink down to rise no more. He saw the forest god or demon rise from the vanquished foe, and placing a foot upon the still quivering carcass, raise his face to the moon and bay out a hideous cry that froze the ebbing blood in the veins of the witch-doctor.

4

Prophecy and Fulfillment

THEN Tarzan turned his attention to the man. He had not slain Numa to save the Negro—he had merely done it in revenge upon the lion; but now that he saw the old man lying helpless and dying before him something akin to pity touched his savage heart. In his youth he would have slain the witch-doctor without the slightest compunction; but civilization had had its softening effect upon him even as it does upon the nations and races which it touches, though it had not yet gone far enough with Tarzan to render him either cowardlly or effeminate. He saw an old man suffering and dying, and he stooped and felt of his wounds and stanched the flow of blood.

"Who are you?" asked the old man in a trembling voice.

"I am Tarzan—Tarzan of the Apes," replied the ape-man and not without a greater touch of pride than he would have said, "I am John Clayton, Lord Greystoke."

The witch-doctor shook convulsively and closed his eyes. When he opened them again there was in them a resignation to whatever horrible fate awaited him at the hands of this feared demon of the woods. "Why do you not kill me?" he asked.

"Why should I kill you?" inquired Tarzan. "You have not harmed me, and anyway you are already dying. Numa, the lion, has killed you."

"You would not kill me?" Surprise and incredulity were in the tones of the quavering old voice.

"I would save you if I could," replied Tarzan, "but that cannot be done. Why did you think I would kill you?"

For a moment the old man was silent. When he spoke it was evidently after some little effort to muster his courage. "I knew you of old," he said, "when you ranged the jungle in the country of Mbonga, the chief. I was already a witch-doctor when you slew Kulonga and the others, and when you robbed our huts and our poison pot. At first I did not remember you; but at last I did—the white-skinned ape that lived with the hairy apes and made life miserable in the village of Mbonga, the chief—the forest god—the Munango-Keewati for whom we set food outside our gates and who came and ate it. Tell me before I die—are you man or devil?"

Tarzan laughed. "I am a man," he said.

The old fellow sighed and shook his head. "You have tried to save me from Simba," he said. "For that I shall reward you. I am a great witch-doctor. Listen to me, white man! I see bad days ahead of you. It is writ in my own blood which I have smeared upon my palm. A god greater even than you will rise up and strike you down. Turn back, Munango-Keewati! Turn back before it is too late. Danger lies ahead of you and danger lurks behind; but greater is the danger before. I see—" He paused and drew a long, gasping breath. Then he crumpled into a little, wrinkled heap and died. Tarzan wondered what else he had seen.

It was very late when the ape-man re-entered the boma and lay down among his black warriors. None had seen him go and none saw him return. He thought about the warning of the old witch-doctor before he fell asleep and he thought of it again after he awoke; but he did not turn back for he was unafraid, though had he known what lay in store for one he loved most in all the world he would have flown through the trees to her side and allowed the gold of Opar to remain forever hidden in its forgotten storehouse.

Behind him that morning another white man pondered something he had heard during the night and very nearly did he give up his project and turn back upon his trail. It was Werper, the murderer, who in the still of the night had heard far away upon the trail ahead of him a sound that had filled his cowardly soul with terror—a sound such as he never before had heard in all his life, nor dreamed that such a frightful thing could emanate from the lungs of a God-created creature. He had heard the victory cry of the bull ape as Tarzan had screamed it forth into the face of Goro, the moon, and he had trembled then and hidden his face; and now in the broad light of a new day he trembled again as he recalled it, and would have turned back from the nameless danger the echo of that frightful sound seemed to portend, had he not stood in even greater fear of Achmet Zek, his master.

And so Tarzan of the Apes forged steadily ahead toward Opar's ruined ramparts and behind him slunk Werper, jackal-like, and only God knew what lay in store for each.

At the edge of the desolate valley, overlooking the golden domes and minarets of Opar, Tarzan halted. By night he would go alone to the treasure vault, reconnoitering, for he had determined that caution should mark his every move upon this expedition.

With the coming of night he set forth, and Werper, who had scaled the cliffs alone behind the ape-man's party, and hidden through the day among the rough boulders of the mountain top, slunk stealthily after him. The boulder-strewn plain between the valley's edge and the mighty granite kopje, outside the city's walls, where lay the entrance to the passage-way leading to the treasure valut, gave the Belgian ample cover as he followed Tarzan toward Opar.

He saw the giant ape-man swing himself nimbly up the face of the great rock. Werper, clawing fearfully during the perilous ascent, sweating in terror, almost palsied by fear, but spurred on by avarice, followed upward, until at last he stood upon the summit of the rocky hill.

Tarzan was nowhere in sight. For a time Werper hid behind one of the lesser boulders that were scattered over the top of the hill, but, seeing or hearing nothing of the Englishman, he crept from his place of concealment to undertake a systematic search of his surroundings, in the hope that he might discover the location of the treasure in ample time to make his escape before Tarzan returned, for it was the Belgian's desire merely to locate the gold, that, after Tarzan had departed, he might come in safety with his followers and carry away as much as he could transport.

He found the narrow cleft leading downward into the heart of the kopje along well-worn, granite steps. He advanced quite to the dark mouth of the tunnel into which the runway disappeared; but here he halted, fearing to enter, lest he meet Tarzan returning.

The ape-man, far ahead of him, groped his way along the rocky passage, until he came to the ancient wooden door. A moment later he stood within the treasure chamber, where, ages since, long-dead hands had ranged the lofty rows of precious ingots for the rulers of that great continent which now lies submerged beneath the waters of the Atlantic.

No sound broke the stillness of the subterranean vault. There was no evidence that another had discovered the forgotten wealth since last the ape-man had visited its hiding place.

Satisfied, Tarzan turned and retraced his steps toward the summit of the kopje. Werper, from the concealment of a jutting, granite shoulder, watched him pass up from the shadows of the stairway and advance toward the edge of the hill which faced the rim of the valley where the Waziri awaited the signal of their master. Then Werper, slipping stealthily from his hiding place, dropped into the somber darkness of the entrance and disappeared.

Tarzan, halting upon the kopje's edge, raised his voice in the thunderous roar of a lion. Twice, at regular intervals, he repeated the call, standing in attentive silence for several minutes after the echoes of the third call had died away. And then, from far across the valley, faintly, came an answering roar—once, twice, thrice. Basuli, the Waziri chieftain, had heard and replied.

Tarzan again made his way toward the treasure vault, knowing that in a few hours his blacks would be with him, ready to bear away another fortune in the strangely shaped, golden ingots of Opar. In the meantime he would carry as much of the precious metal to the summit of the kopje as he could.

Six trips he made in the five hours before Basuli reached the kopje, and at the end of that time he had transported forty-eight ingots to the edge of the great boulder, carrying upon each trip a load which might well have staggered two ordinary men, yet his giant frame showed no evidence of fatigue, as he helped to raise his ebon warriors to the hill top with the rope that had been brought for the purpose.

Six times he had returned to the treasure chamber, and six times Werper, the Belgian, had cowered in the black shadows at the far end of the long vault. Once again came the ape-man, and this time there came with him fifty fighting men, turned porters for love of the only creature in the world who might command of their fierce and haughty natures such menial service. Fifty-two more ingots passed out of the vaults, making the total of one hundred which Tarzan intended taking away with him.

As the last of the Waziri filed from the chamber, Tarzan turned back for a last glimpse of the fabulous wealth upon which his two inroads had made no appreciable impression. Before he extinguished the single candle he had brought with him for the purpose, and the flickering light of which had cast the first alleviating rays into the impenetrable darkness of the buried chamber, that it had known for the countless ages since it had lain forgotten of man, Tarzan's mind reverted to that first occasion upon which he had entered the treasure vault, coming upon it by chance as he fled from the pits beneath the temple, where he had been hidden by La, the High Priestess of the Sun Worshipers.

He recalled the scene within the temple when he had lain stretched upon the sacrificial altar, while La, with high-raised dagger, stood above him, and the rows of priests and priestesses awaited, in the ecstatic hysteria of fanaticism, the first gush of their victim's warm blood, that they might fill their golden goblets and drink to the glory of their Flaming God.

The brutal and bloody interruption by Tha, the mad priest, passed vividly before the ape-man's recollective eye, the flight of the votaries before the insane blood lust of the hideous creature, the brutal attack upon La, and his own part in the grim tragedy when he had battled with the infuriated Oparian and left him dead at the feet of the priestess he would have profaned.

This and much more passed through Tarzan's memory as he stood gazing at the long tiers of dull-yellow metal. He wondered if La still ruled in the temples of the ruined city whose crumbling walls rose upon the very foundations about him. Had she finally been forced into a union with one of her grotesque priests? It seemed a hideous fate, indeed, for one so beautiful. With a shake of his head, Tarzan stepped to the flickering candle, extinguished its feeble rays and turned toward the exit.

Behind him the spy waited for him to be gone. He had

learned the secret for which he had come, and now he could return at his leisure to his waiting followers, bring them to the treasure vault and carry away all the gold that they could stagger under.

The Waziri had reached the outer end of the tunnel, and were winding upward toward the fresh air and the welcome starlight of the kopje's summit, before Tarzan shook off the detaining hand of reverie and started slowly after them.

Once again, and, he thought, for the last time, he closed the massive door of the treasure room. In the darkness behind him Werper rose and stretched his cramped muscles. He stretched forth a hand and lovingly caressed a golden ingot on the nearest tier. He raised it from its immemorial resting place and weighed it in his hands. He clutched it to his bosom in an ecstasy of avarice.

Tarzan dreamed of the happy homecoming which lay before him, of dear arms about his neck, and a soft cheek pressed to his; but there rose to dispel that dream the memory of the old witch-doctor and his warning.

And then, in the span of a few brief seconds, the hopes of both these men were shattered. The one forgot even his greed in the panic of terror—the other was plunged into total forgetfulness of the past by a jagged fragment of rock which gashed a deep cut upon his head.

5

The Altar of the Flaming God

I T WAS at the moment that Tarzan turned from the closed door to pursue his way to the outer world. The thing came without warning. One instant all was quiet and stability—the next, and the world rocked, the tortured sides of the narrow passageway split and crumbled, great blocks of granite, dislodged from the ceiling, tumbled into the narrow way, choking it, and the walls bent inward upon the wreckage. Beneath the blow of a fragment of the roof, Tarzan staggered back against the door to the treasure room, his weight pushed it open and his body rolled inward upon the floor.

In the great apartment where the treasure lay less damage was wrought by the earthquake. A few ingots toppled from the higher tiers, a single piece of the rocky ceiling splintered off and crashed downward to the floor, and the walls cracked, though they did not collapse.

There was but the single shock, no other followed to complete the damage undertaken by the first. Werper, thrown to his length by the suddenness and violence of the disturbance, staggered to his feet when he found himself unhurt. Groping his way toward the far end of the chamber, he sought the candle which Tarzan had left stuck in its own wax upon the protruding end of an ingot.

By striking numerous matches the Belgian at last found what he sought, and when, a moment later, the sickly rays relieved the Stygian darkness about him, he breathed a nervous sigh of relief, for the impenetrable gloom had accentuated the terrors of his situation.

As they became accustomed to the light the man turned his eyes toward the door—his one thought now was of escape from this frightful tomb—and as he did so he saw the body of the naked giant lying stretched upon the floor just within the doorway. Werper drew back in sudden fear of detection; but a second glance convinced him that the Englishman was dead. From a great gash in the man's head a pool of blood had collected upon the concrete floor.

Quickly, the Belgian leaped over the prostrate form of his erstwhile host, and without a thought of succor for the man in whom, for aught he knew, life still remained, he bolted for the passageway and safety.

But his renewed hopes were soon dashed. Just beyond the doorway he found the passage completely clogged and choked by impenetrable masses of shattered rock. Once more he turned and re-entered the treasure vault. Taking the candle from its place he commenced a systematic search of the apartment, nor had he gone far before he discovered another door in the opposite end of the room, a door which gave upon creaking hinges to the weight of his body. Beyond the door lay another narrow passageway. Along this Werper made his way, ascending a flight of stone steps to another corridor twenty feet above the level of the first. The flickering candle lighted the way before him, and a moment later he was thankful for the possession of this crude and antiquated luminant, which, a few hours before he might have looked upon with contempt, for it showed him, just in time, a yawning pit, apparently terminating the tunnel he was traversing.

Before him was a circular shaft. He held the candle above it and peered downward. Below him, at a great distance, he saw the light reflected back from the surface of a pool of water. He had come upon a well. He raised the candle above his head and peered across the black void, and there upon the opposite side he saw the continuation of the tunnel; but how was he to span the gulf?

As he stood there measuring the distance to the opposite side and wondering if he dared venture so great a leap, there broke suddenly upon his startled ears a piercing scream which diminished gradually until it ended in a series of dismal moans. The voice seemed partly human, yet so hideous that it might well have emanated from the tortured throat of a lost soul, writhing in the fires of hell.

The Belgian shuddered and looked fearfully upward, for the scream had seemed to come from above him. As he looked he saw an opening far overhead, and a patch of sky pinked with brilliant stars.

His half-formed intention to call for help was expunged by the terrifying cry—where such a voice lived, no human creatures could dwell. He dared not reveal himself to whatever inhabitants dwelt in the place above him. He cursed himself for a fool that he had ever embarked upon such a mission. He wished himself safely back in the camp of Achmet Zek, and would almost have embraced an opportunity to give himself up to the military authorities of the Congo if by so doing he might be rescued from the frightful predicament in which he now was.

He listened fearfully, but the cry was not repeated, and at last spurred to desperate means, he gathered himself for the leap across the chasm. Going back twenty paces, he took a running start, and at the edge of the well, leaped upward and outward in an attempt to gain the opposite side.

In his hand he clutched the sputtering candle, and as he took the leap the rush of air extinguished it. In utter darkness he flew through space, clutching outward for a hold should his feet miss the invisible ledge.

He struck the edge of the floor of the opposite terminus of the rocky tunnel with his knees, slipped backward, clutched desperately for a moment, and at last hung half within and half without the opening; but he was safe. For several minutes he dared not move; but clung, weak and sweating, where he lay. At last, cautiously, he drew himself well within the tunnel, and again he lay at full length upon the floor, fighting to regain control of his shattered nerves.

When his knees struck the edge of the tunnel he had dropped the candle. Presently, hoping against hope that it had fallen upon the floor of the passageway, rather than back into the depths of the well, he rose upon all fours and commenced a diligent search for the little tallow cylinder, which now seemed infinitely more precious to him than all the fabulous wealth of the hoarded ingots of Opar.

And when, at last, he found it, he clasped it to him and sank back sobbing and exhausted. For many minutes he lay trembling and broken; but finally he drew himself to a sitting posture, and taking a match from his pocket, lighted the stump of the candle which remained to him. With the light he found it easier to regain control of his nerves, and presently he was again making his way along the tunnel in search of an avenue of escape. The horrid cry that had come down to him from above through the ancient well-shaft still haunted him, so that he trembled in terror at even the sounds of his own cautious advance.

He had gone forward but a short distance, when, to his chagrin, a wall of masonry barred his farther progress, closing the tunnel completely from top to bottom and from side to side. What could it mean? Werper was an educated and intelligent man. His military training had taught him to use his mind for the purpose for which it was intended. A blind tunnel such as this was senseless. It must continue beyond the wall. Someone, at some time in the past, had had it blocked for an unknown purpose of his own. The man fell to examining the masonry by the light of his candle. To his delight he discovered that the thin blocks of hewn stone of which it was constructed were fitted in loosely without mortar or cement. He tugged upon one of them, and to his joy found that it was easily removable. One after another he pulled out the blocks until he had opened an aperture large enough to admit his body, then he crawled through into a large, low chamber. Across this another door barred his way; but this, too, gave before his efforts, for it was not barred. A long, dark corridor showed before him, but before he had followed it far, his candle burned down until it scorched his fingers. With an oath he dropped it to the floor, where it sputtered for a moment and went out.

Now he was in total darkness, and again terror rode heavily astride his neck. What further pitfalls and dangers lay ahead he could not guess; but that he was as far as ever from liberty he was quite willing to believe, so depressing is utter absence of light to one in unfamiliar surroundings.

Slowly he groped his way along, feeling with his hands upon the tunnel's walls, and cautiously with his feet ahead of him upon the floor before he would take a single forward step. How long he crept on thus he could not guess; but at last, feeling that the tunnel's length was interminable, and exhausted by his efforts, by terror, and loss of sleep, he determined to lie down and rest before proceeding farther.

When he awoke there was no change in the surrounding blackness. He might have slept a second or a day—he could not know; but that he had slept for some time was attested by the fact that he felt refreshed and hungry.

Again he commenced his groping advance; but this time he had gone but a short distance when he emerged into a room, which was lighted through an opening in the ceiling, from which a flight of concrete steps led downward to the floor of the chamber.

Above him, through the aperture, Werper could see sunlight glancing from massive columns, which were twined about by clinging vines. He listened; but he heard no sound other than the soughing of the wind through leafy branches, the hoarse cries of birds, and the chattering of monkeys.

Boldly he ascended the stairway, to find himself in a circular court. Just before him stood a stone altar, stained with rusty-brown discolorations. At the time Werper gave no thought to an explanation of these stains—later their origin became all too hideously apparent to him.

Besides the opening in the floor, just behind the altar, through which he had entered the court from the subterranean chamber below, the Belgian discovered several doors leading from the enclosure upon the level of the floor. Above, and circling the courtyard, was a series of open balconies. Monkeys scampered about the deserted ruins, and gaily plumaged birds flitted in and out among the columns and the galleries far above; but no sign of human presence was discernible. Werper felt relieved. He sighed, as though a great weight had been lifted from his shoulders. He took a step toward one of the exits, and then he halted, wideeyed in astonishment and terror, for almost at the same instant a dozen doors opened in the courtyard wall and a horde of frightful men rushed in upon him.

They were the priests of the Flaming God of Opar—the same, shaggy, knotted, hideous little men who had dragged Jane Clayton to the sacrificial altar at this very spot years before. Their long arms, their short and crooked legs, their close-set, evil eyes, and their low, receding foreheads gave them a bestial appearance that sent a qualm of paralyzing fright through the shaken nerves of the Belgian.

With a scream he turned to flee back into the lesser terrors of the gloomy corridors and apartments from which he had just emerged, but the frightful men anticipated his intentions. They blocked the way; they seized him, and though he fell, groveling upon his knees before them, begging for his life, they bound him and hurled him to the floor of the inner temple.

The rest was but a repetition of what Tarzan and Jane Clayton had passed through. The priestesses came, and with them La, the High Priestess. Werper was raised and laid across the altar. Cold sweat exuded from his every pore as La raised the cruel, sacrificial knife above him. The death chant fell upon his tortured ears. His staring eyes wandered to the golden goblets from which the hideous votaries would soon quench their inhuman thirst in his own, warm life-blood.

He wished that he might be granted the brief respite of unconsciousness before the final plunge of the keen blade—and then there was a frightful roar that sounded almost in his ears. The High Priestess lowered her dagger. Her eyes went wide in horror. The priestesses, her votaresses, screamed and fled madly toward the exits. The priests roared out their rage and terror according to the temper of their courage. Werper strained his neck about to catch a sight of the cause of their panic, and when, at last he saw it, he too went cold in dread, for what his eyes beheld was the figure of a huge lion standing in the center of the temple, and already a single victim lay mangled beneath his cruel paws.

Again the lord of the wilderness roared, turning his baleful gaze upon the altar. La staggered forward, reeled, and fell across Werper in a swoon.

6

The Arab Raid

AFTER their first terror had subsided subsequent to the shock of the earthquake, Basuli and his warriors hastened back into the passageway in search of Tarzan and two of their own number who were also missing.

They found the way blocked by jammed and distorted rock. For two days they labored to tear a way through to their imprisoned friends; but when, after Herculean efforts, they had unearthed but a few yards of the choked passage, and discovered the mangled remains of one of their fellows they were forced to the conclusion that Tarzan and the second Waziri also lay dead beneath the rock mass farther in, beyond human aid, and no longer susceptible of it.

Again and again as they labored they called aloud the names of their master and their comrade; but no answering call rewarded their listening ears. At last they gave up the search. Tearfully they cast a last look at the shattered tomb of their master, shouldered the heavy burden of gold that would at least furnish comfort, if not happiness, to their bereaved and beloved mistress, and made their mournful way back across the desolate valley of Opar, and downward through the forests beyond toward the distant bungalow.

And as they marched what sorry fate was already drawing down upon that peaceful, happy home!

From the north came Achmet Zek, riding to the summons of his lieutenant's letter. With him came his horde of renegade Arabs, outlawed marauders, these, and equally degraded blacks, garnered from the more debased and ignorant tribes of savage cannibals through whose countries the raider passed to and fro with perfect impunity.

Mugambi, the ebon Hercules, who had shared the dangers and vicissitudes of his beloved Bwana, from Jungle Island, almost to the headwaters of the Ugambi, was the first to note the bold approach of the sinister caravan.

He it was whom Tarzan had left in charge of the warriors who remained to guard Lady Greystoke, nor could a braver or more loyal guardian have been found in any clime or upon any soil. A giant in stature, a savage, fearless warrior, the huge black possessed also soul and judgment in proportion to his bulk and his ferocity.

Not once since his master had departed had he been beyond sight or sound of the bungalow, except when Lady Greystoke chose to canter across the broad plain, or relieve the monotony of her loneliness by a brief hunting excursion. On such occasions Mugambi, mounted upon a wiry Arab, had ridden close at her horse's heels.

The raiders were still a long way off when the warrior's keen eyes discovered them. For a time he stood scrutinizing the advancing party in silence, then he turned and ran rapidly in the direction of the native huts which lay a few hundred yards below the bungalow.

Here he called out to the lolling warriors. He issued orders rapidly. In compliance with them the men seized upon their weapons and their shields. Some ran to call in the workers from the fields and to warn the tenders of the flocks and herds. The majority followed Mugambi back toward the bungalow.

The dust of the raiders was still a long distance away.

Mugambi could not know positively that it hid an enemy; but he had spent a lifetime of savage life in savage Africa, and he had seen parties before come thus unheralded. Sometimes they had come in peace and sometimes they had come in war—one could never tell. It was well to be prepared. Mugambi did not like the haste with which the strangers advanced.

The Greystoke bungalow was not well adapted for defense. No palisade surrounded it, for, situated as it was, in the heart of loyal Waziri, its master had anticipated no possibility of an attack in force by any enemy. Heavy, wooden shutters there were to close the window apertures against hostile arrows, and these Mugambi was engaged in lowering when Lady Greystoke appeared upon the veranda.

"Why, Mugambi!" she exclaimed. "What has happened? Why are you lowering the shutters?"

Mugambi pointed out across the plain to where a white-robed force of mounted men was now distinctly visible.

"Arabs," he explained. "They come for no good purpose in the absence of the Great Bwana."

Beyond the neat lawn and the flowering shrubs, Jane Clayton saw the glistening bodies of her Waziri. The sun glanced from the tips of their metal-shod spears, picked out the gorgeous colors in the feathers of their war bonnets, and reflected the high-lights from the glossy skins of their broad shoulders and high cheek bones.

Jane Clayton surveyed them with unmixed feelings of pride and affection. What harm could befall her with such as these to protect her?

The raiders had halted now, a hundred yards out upon the plain. Mugambi had hastened down to join his warriors. He advanced a few yards before them and raising his voice hailed the strangers. Achmet Zek sat straight in his saddle before his henchmen.

"Arab!" cried Mugambi. "What do you here?"

"We come in peace," Achmet Zek called back.

"Then turn and go in peace," replied Mugambi. "We do not want you here. There can be no peace between Arab and Waziri."

Mugambi, although not born a Waziri, had been adopted into the tribe, which now contained no member more jealous of its traditions and its prowess than he.

Achmet Zek drew to one side of his horde, speaking to his men in a low voice. A moment later, without warning, a ragged volley was poured into the ranks of the Waziri. A couple of the warriors fell, the others were for charging the attackers; but Mugambi was a cautious as well as a brave leader. He knew the futility of charging mounted men armed with muskets. He withdrew his force behind the shrubbery of the garden. Some he dispatched to various other parts of the grounds surrounding the bungalow. Half a dozen he sent to the bungalow itself with instructions to keep their mistress within doors, and to protect her with their lives.

Adopting the tactics of the desert fighters from which he had sprung, Achmet Zek led his followers at a gallop in a long, thin line, describing a great circle which drew closer and closer in toward the defenders.

At that part of the circle closest to the Waziri, a constant fusillade of shots was poured into the bushes behind which the black warriors had concealed themselves. The latter, on their part, loosed their slim shafts at the nearest of the enemy.

The Waziri, justly famed for their archery, found no cause to blush for their performance that day. Time and again some swarthy horseman threw hands above his head and toppled from his saddle, pierced by a deadly arrow; but the contest was uneven. The Arabs outnumbered the Waziri; their bullets penetrated the shrubbery and found marks that the Arab riflemen had not even seen; and then Achmet Zek circled inward a half mile above the bungalow, tore down a section of the fence, and led his marauders within the grounds.

Across the fields they charged at a mad run. Not again did they pause to lower fences, instead, they drove their wild mounts straight for them, clearing the obstacles as lightly as winged gulls.

Mugambi saw them coming, and, calling those of his warriors who remained, ran for the bungalow and the last stand. Upon the veranda Lady Greystoke stood, rifle in hand. More than a single raider had accounted to her steady nerves and cool aim for his outlawry; more than a single pony raced, riderless, in the wake of the charging horde.

Mugambi pushed his mistress back into the greater security of the interior, and with his depleted force prepared to make a last stand against the foe.

On came the Arabs, shouting and waving their long guns above their heads. Past the veranda they raced, pouring a deadly fire into the kneeling Waziri who discharged their volley of arrows from behind their long, oval shields—shields well adapted, perhaps, to stop a hostile arrow, or deflect a spear; but futile, quite, before the leaden missiles of the riflemen.

From beneath the half-raised shutters of the bungalow

other bowmen did effective service in greater security, and
after the first assault, Mugambi withdrew his entire force
within the building.

Again and again the Arabs charged, at last forming a
stationary circle about the little fortress, and outside the
effective range of the defenders' arrows. From their new position they fired at will at the windows. One by one the
Waziri fell. Fewer and fewer were the arrows that replied
to the gungs of the raiders, and at last Achmet Zek felt safe
in ordering an assault.

Firing as they ran, the bloodthirsty horde raced for the
veranda. A dozen of them fell to the arrows of the defenders; but the majority reached the door. Heavy gun butts
fell upon it. The crash of splintered wood mingled with the
report of a rifle as Jane Clayton fired through the panels
upon the relentless foe.

Upon both sides of the door men fell; but at last the
frail barrier gave to the vicious assaults of the maddened attackers; it crumpled inward and a dozen swarthy murder-
ers leaped into the living-room. At the far end stood Jane
Clayton surrounded by the remnant of her devoted guard-
ians. The floor was covered by the bodies of those who already had given up their lives in her defense. In the fore-
front of her protectors stood the giant Mugambi. The Arabs
raised their rifles to pour in the last volley that would
effectually end all resistance; but Achmet Zek roared out a
warning order that stayed their trigger fingers.

"Fire not upon the woman!" he cried. "Who harms her,
dies. Take the woman alive!"

The Arabs rushed across the room; the Waziri met them
with their heavy spears. Swords flashed, long-barreled pis-
tols roared out their sullen death dooms. Mugambi launched
his spear at the nearest of the enemy with a force that
drove the heavy shaft completely through the Arab's body,
then he seized a pistol from another, and grasping it by the
barrel brained all who forced their way too near his mistress.

Emulating his example the few warriors who remained to
him fought like demons; but one by one they fell, until only
Mugambi remained to defend the life and honor of the
ape-man's mate.

From across the room Achmet Zek watched the unequal
struggle and urged on his minions. In his hands was a
jeweled musket. Slowly he raised it to his shoulder, waiting
until another move should place Mugambi at his mercy
without endangering the lives of the woman or any of his
own followers.

At last the moment came, and Achmet Zek pulled the trigger. Without a sound the brave Mugambi sank to the floor at the feet of Jane Clayton.

An instant later she was surrounded and disarmed. Without a word they dragged her from the bungalow. A giant Negro lifted her to the pommel of his saddle, and while the raiders searched the bungalow and outhouses for plunder he rode with her beyond the gates and waited the coming of his master.

Jane Clayton saw the raiders lead the horses from the corral, and drive the herds in from the fields. She saw her home plundered of all that represented intrinsic worth in the eyes of the Arabs, and then she saw the torch applied, and the flames lick up what remained.

And at last, when the raiders assembled after glutting their fury and their avarice, and rode away with her toward the north, she saw the smoke and the flames rising far into the heavens until the winding of the trail into the thick forests hid the sad view from her eyes.

As the flames ate their way into the living-room, reaching out forked tongues to lick up the bodies of the dead, one of that gruesome company whose bloody welterings had long since been stilled, moved again. It was a huge black who rolled over upon his side and opened blood-shot, suffering eyes. Mugambi, whom the Arabs had left for dead, still lived. The hot flames were almost upon him as he raised himself painfully upon his hands and knees and crawled slowly toward the doorway.

Again and again he sank weakly to the floor; but each time he rose again and continued his pitiful way toward safety. After what seemed to him an interminable time, during which the flames had become a veritable fiery furnace at the far side of the room, the great black managed to reach the veranda, roll down the steps, and crawl off into the cool safety of some nearby shrubbery.

All night he lay there, alternately unconscious and painfully sentient; and in the latter state watching with savage hatred the lurid flames which still rose from burning crib and hay cock. A prowling lion roared close at hand; but the giant black was unafraid. There was place for but a single thought in his savage mind—revenge! revenge! revenge!

7

The Jewel-Room of Opar

FOR some time Tarzan lay where he had fallen upon the floor of the treasure chamber beneath the ruined walls of Opar. He lay as one dead; but he was not dead. At length he stirred. His eyes opened upon the utter darkness of the room. He raised his hand to his head and brought it away sticky with clotted blood. He sniffed at his fingers, as a wild beast might sniff at the life-blood upon a wounded paw.

Slowly he rose to a sitting posture—listening. No sound reached to the buried depths of his sepulcher. He staggered to his feet, and groped his way about among the tiers of ingots. What was he? Where was he? His head ached; but otherwise he felt no ill effects from the blow that had felled him. The accident he did not recall, nor did he recall aught of what had led up to it.

He let his hands grope unfamiliarly over his limbs, his torso, and his head. He felt of the quiver at his back, the knife in his loin cloth. Something struggled for recognition within his brain. Ah! he had it. There was something missing. He crawled about upon the floor, feeling with his hands for the thing that instinct warned him was gone. At last he found it—the heavy war spear that in past years had formed so important a feature of his daily life, almost of his very existence, so inseparably had it been connected with his every action since the long-gone day that he had wrested his first spear from the body of a black victim of his savage training.

Tarzan was sure that there was another and more lovely world than that which was confined to the darkness of the four stone walls surrounding him. He continued his search and at last found the doorway leading inward beneath the city and the temple. This he followed, most incautiously. He came to the stone steps leading upward to the higher level. He ascended them and continued onward toward the well.

Nothing spurred his hurt memory to a recollection of past familiarity with his surroundings. He blundered on through the darkness as though he were traversing an open plain under the brilliance of a noonday sun, and suddenly there happened that which had to happen under the circumstances of his rash advance.

He reached the brink of the well, stepped outward into space, lunged forward, and shot downward into the inky depths below. Still clutching his spear, he struck the water, and sank beneath its surface, plumming the depths.

The fall had not injured him, and when he rose to the surface, he shook the water from his eyes, and found that he could see. Daylight was filtering into the well from the orifice far above his head. It illumined the inner walls faintly. Tarzan gazed about him. On the level with the surface of the water he saw a large opening in the dark and slimy wall. He swam to it, and drew himself out upon the wet floor of a tunnel.

Along this he passed; but now he went warily, for Tarzan of the Apes was learning. The unexpected pit had taught him care in the traversing of dark passageways—he needed no second lesson.

For a long distance the passage went straight as an arrow. The floor was slippery, as though at times the rising waters of the well overflowed and flooded it. This, in itself, retarded Tarzan's pace, for it was with difficulty that he kept his footing.

The foot of a stairway ended the passage. Up this he made his way. It turned back and forth many times, leading, at last, into a small, circular chamber, the gloom of which was relieved by a faint light which found ingress through a tubular shaft several feet in diameter which rose from the center of the room's ceiling, upward to a distance of a hundred feet or more, where it terminated in a stone grating through which Tarzan could see a blue and sun-lit sky.

Curiosity prompted the ape-man to investigate his surroundings. Several metal-bound, copper-studded chests constituted the sole furniture of the round room. Tarzan let his hands run over these. He felt of the copper studs, he pulled upon the hinges, and at last, by chance, he raised the cover of one.

An exclamation of delight broke from his lips at sight of the pretty contents. Gleaming and glistening in the subdued light of the chamber, lay a great tray full of brilliant stones. Tarzan, reverted to the primitive by his accident, had no conception of the fabulous value of his find. To him they were but pretty pebbles. He plunged his hands into them and let the priceless gems filter through his fingers. He went to others of the chests, only to find still further stores of precious stones. Nearly all were cut, and from these he gathered a handful and filled the pouch which dangled at his side—the uncut stones he tossed back into the chests.

Unwittingly, the ape-man had stumbled upon the forgotten jewel-room of Opar. For ages it had lain buried beneath the temple of the Flaming God, midway of one of the many inky passages which the superstitious descendants of the ancient Sun Worshipers had either dared not or cared not to explore.

Tiring at last of this diversion, Tarzan took up his way along the corridor which led upward from the jewel-room by a steep incline. Winding and twisting, but always tending upward, the tunnel led him nearer and nearer to the surface, ending finally in a low-ceiled room, lighter than any that he had as yet discovered.

Above him an opening in the ceiling at the upper end of a flight of concrete steps revealed a brilliant sunlit scene. Tarzan viewed the vine-covered columns in mild wonderment. He puckered his brows in an attempt to recall some recollection of similar things. He was not sure of himself. There was a tantalizing suggestion always present in his mind that something was eluding him—that he should know many things which he did not know.

His earnest cogitation was rudely interrupted by a thunderous roar from the opening above him. Following the roar came the cries and screams of men and women. Tarzan grasped his spear more firmly and ascended the steps. A strange sight met his eyes as he emerged from the semi-darkness of the cellar to the brilliant light of the temple.

The creatures he saw before him he recognized for what they were—men and women, and a huge lion. The men and women were scuttling for the safety of the exits. The lion stood upon the body of one who had been less fortunate than the others. He was in the center of the temple. Directly before Tarzan, a woman stood beside a block of stone. Upon the top of the stone lay stretched a man, and as the ape-man watched the scene, he saw the lion glare terribly at the two who remained within the temple. Another thunderous roar broke from the savage throat, the woman screamed and swooned across the body of the man stretched prostrate upon the stone altar before her.

The lion advanced a few steps and crouched. The tip of his sinuous tail twitched nervously. He was upon the point of charging when his eyes were attracted toward the ape-man.

Werper, helpless upon the altar, saw the great carnivore

preparing to leap upon him. He saw the sudden change in the beast's expression as his eyes wandered to something beyond the altar and out of the Belgian's view. He saw the formidable creature rise to a standing position. A figure darted past Werper. He saw a mighty arm upraised, and a stout spear shoot forward toward the lion, to bury itself in the broad chest.

He saw the lion snapping and tearing at the weapon's shaft, and he saw, wonder of wonders, the naked giant who had hurled the missle charging upon the great beast, only a long knife ready to meet those ferocious fangs and talons.

The lion reared up to meet this new enemy. The beast was growling frightfully, and then upon the startled ears of the Belgian, broke a similar savage growl from the lips of the man rushing upon the beast.

By a quick side step, Tarzan eluded the first swinging clutch of the lion's paws. Darting to the beast's side, he leaped upon the tawny back. His arms encircled the maned neck, his teeth sank deep into the brute's flesh. Roaring, leaping, rolling and struggling, the giant cat attempted to dislodge this savage enemy, and all the while one great, brown fist was driving a long keen blade repeatedly into the beast's side.

During the battle, La regained consciousness. Spellbound, she stood above her victim watching the spectacle. It seemed incredible that a human being could best the king of beasts in personal encounter and yet before her very eyes there was taking place just such an improbability.

At last Tarzan's knife found the great heart, and with a final, spasmodic struggle the lion rolled over upon the marble floor, dead. Leaping to his feet the conqueror placed a foot upon the carcass of his kill, raised his face toward the heavens, and gave voice to so hideous a cry that both La and Werper trembled as it reverberated through the temple.

Then the ape-man turned, and Werper recognized him as the man he had left for dead in the treasure room.

WERPER was astounded. Could this creature be the same dignified Englishman who had entertained him so graciously in his luxurious African home? Could this wild beast, with blazing eyes, and bloody countenance, be at the same time a man? Could the horrid, victory cry he had but just heard have been formed in human throat?

Tarzan was eyeing the man and the woman, a puzzled expression in his eyes, but there was no faintest tinge of recognition. It was as though he had discovered some new species of living creature and was marveling at his find.

La was studying the ape-man's features. Slowly her large eyes opened very wide.

"Tarzan!" she exclaimed, and then, in the vernacular of the great apes which constant association with the anthropoids had rendered the common language of the Oparians: "You have come back to me! La has ignored the mandates of her religion, waiting, always waiting for Tarzan—for her Tarzan. She has taken no mate, for in all the world there was but one with whom La would mate. And now you have come back! Tell me, O Tarzan, that it is for me you have returned."

Werper listened to the unintelligible jargon. He looked from La to Tarzan. Would the latter understand this strange tongue? To the Belgian's surprise, the Englishman answered in a language evidently identical to hers.

"Tarzan," he repeated, musingly. "Tarzan. The name sounds familiar."

"It is your name—you are Tarzan," cried La.

"I am Tarzan?" The ape-man shrugged. "Well, it is a good name—I know no other, so I will keep it; but I do not know you. I did not come hither for you. Why I came, I do not know at all; neither do I know from whence I came. Can you tell me?"

La shook her head. "I never knew," she replied.

Tarzan turned toward Werper and put the same question to him; but in the language of the great apes. The Belgian shook his head.

"I do not understand that language," he said in French.

Without effort, and apparently without realizing that he made the change, Tarzan repeated his question in French. Werper suddenly came to a full realization of the magnitude of the injury of which Tarzan was a victim. The man had lost his memory—no longer could he recollect past events. The Belgian was upon the point of enlightening him, when it suddenly occurred to him that by keeping Tarzan in ignorance, for a time at least, of his true identity, it might be possible to turn the ape-man's misfortune to his own advantage.

"I cannot tell you from whence you came," he said; "but this I can tell you—if we do not get out of this horrible place we shall both be slain upon this bloody altar. The woman was about to plunge her knife into my heart when the lion interrupted the fiendish ritual. Come! Before they recover from their fright and reassemble, let us find a way out of their damnable temple."

Tarzan turned again toward La.

"Why," he asked, "would you have killed this man? Are you hungry?"

The High Priestess cried out in disgust.

"Did he attempt to kill you?" continued Tarzan.

The woman shook her head.

"Then why should you have wished to kill him?" Tarzan was determined to get to the bottom of the thing.

La raised her slender arm and pointed toward the sun.

"We were offering up his soul as a gift to the Flaming God," she said.

Tarzan looked puzzled. He was again an ape, and apes do not understand such matters as souls and Flaming Gods.

"Do you wish to die?" he asked Werper.

The Belgian assured him, with tears in his eyes, that he did not wish to die.

"Very well then, you shall not," said Tarzan. "Come! We will go. This *she* would kill you and keep me for herself. It is no place anyway for a Mangani. I should soon die, shut up behind these stone walls."

He turned toward La. "We are going now," he said.

The woman rushed forward and seized the ape-man's hands in hers.

"Do not leave me!" she cried. "Stay, and you shall be High Priest. La loves you. All Opar shall be yours. Slaves shall wait upon you. Stay, Tarzan of the Apes, and let love reward you."

The ape-man pushed the kneeling woman aside. "Tarzan does not desire you," he said, simply, and stepping to Werper's side he cut the Belgian's bonds and motioned him to follow.

Panting—her face convulsed with rage, La sprang to her feet.

"Stay, you shall!" she screamed. "La will have you—if she cannot have you alive, she will have you dead," and raising her face to the sun she gave voice to the same hideous shriek that Werper had heard once before and Tarzan many times.

In answer to her cry a babel of voices broke from the surrounding chambers and corridors.

"Come, Guardian Priests!" she cried. "The infidels have profaned the holiest of the holies. Come! Strike terror to their hearts; defend La and her altar; wash clean the temple with the blood of the polluters."

Tarzan understood, though Werper did not. The former glanced at the Belgian and saw that he was unarmed. Stepping quickly to La's side the ape-man seized her in his strong arms and though she fought with all the mad savagery of a demon, he soon disarmed her, handing her long, sacrificial knife to Werper.

"You will need this," he said, and then from each doorway a horde of the monstrous, little men of Opar streamed into the temple.

They were armed with bludgeons and knives, and fortified in their courage by fanatical hate and frenzy. Werper was terrified. Tarzan stood eyeing the foe in proud disdain. Slowly he advanced toward the exit he had chosen to utilize in making his way from the temple. A burly priest barred his way. Behind the first was a score of others. Tarzan swung his heavy spear, clublike, down upon the skull of the priest. The fellow collapsed, his head crushed.

Again and again the weapon fell as Tarzan made his way slowly toward the doorway. Werper pressed close behind, casting backward glances toward the shrieking, dancing mob menacing their rear. He held the sacrificial knife ready to strike whoever might come within its reach; but none came. For a time he wondered that they should so bravely battle with the giant ape-man, yet hesitate to rush upon him, who was relatively so weak. Had they done so he knew that he must have fallen at the first charge. Tarzan had reached the doorway over the corpses of all that had stood to dispute his way, before Werper guessed at the reason for his immunity. The priests feared the sacrificial knife! Willingly would they face death and welcome it if it came while they defended their High Priestess and her altar; but evidently there were deaths, and deaths. Some strange superstition must surround that polished blade, that no Oparian cared to chance a death thrust from it, yet gladly rushed to the slaughter of the ape-man's flaying spear.

Once outside the temple court, Werper communicated his discovery to Tarzan. The ape-man grinned, and let Werper go before him, brandishing the jeweled and holy weapon. Like leaves before a gale, the Oparians scattered in all directions and Tarzan and the Belgian found a clear passage through the corridors and chambers of the ancient temple.

The Belgian's eyes went wide as they passed through the room of the seven pillars of solid gold. With ill-concealed avarice he looked upon the age-old, golden tablets set in the walls of nearly every room and down the sides of many of the corridors. To the ape-man all this wealth appeared to mean nothing.

On the two went, chance leading them toward the broad avenue which lay between the stately piles of the half-ruined edifices and the inner wall of the city. Great apes jabbered at them and menaced them; but Tarzan answered them after their own kind, giving back taunt for taunt, insult for insult, challenge for challenge.

Werper saw a hairy bull swing down from a broken column and advance, stiff-legged and bristling, toward the naked giant. The yellow fangs were bared, angry snarls and barkings rumbled threateningly through the thick and hanging lips.

The Belgian watched his companion. To his horror, he saw the man stoop until his closed knuckles rested upon the ground as did those of the anthropoid. He saw him circle, stiff-legged about the circling ape. He heard the same bestial barkings and growlings issue from the human throat that were coming from the mouth of the brute. Had his eyes been closed he could not have known but that two giant apes were bridling for combat.

But there was no battle. It ended as the majority of such jungle encounters end—one of the boasters loses his nerve, and becomes suddenly interested in a blowing leaf, a beetle, or the lice upon his hairy stomach.

In this instance it was the anthropoid that retired in stiff dignity to inspect an unhappy caterpillar, which he presently devoured. For a moment Tarzan seemed inclined to pursue the argument. He swaggered truculently, stuck out his chest, roared and advanced closer to the bull. It was with difficulty that Werper finally persuaded him to leave well enough alone and continue his way from the ancient city of the Sun Worshipers.

The two searched for nearly an hour before they found

the narrow exit through the inner wall. From there the well-worn trail led them beyond the outer fortification to the desolate valley of Opar.

Tarzan had no idea, in so far as Werper could discover, as to where he was or whence he came. He wandered aimlessly about, searching for food, which he discovered beneath small rocks, or hiding in the shade of the scant brush which dotted the ground.

The Belgian was horrified by the hideous menu of his companion. Beetles, rodents and caterpillars were devoured with seeming relish. Tarzan was indeed an ape again.

At last Werper succeeded in leading his companion toward the distant hills which mark the northwestern boundary of the valley, and together the two set out in the direction of the Greystoke bungalow.

What purpose prompted the Belgian in leading the victim of his treachery and greed back toward his former home it is difficult to guess, unless it was that without Tarzan there could be no ransom for Tarzan's wife.

That night they camped in the valley beyond the hills, and as they sat before a little fire where cooked a wild pig that had fallen to one of Tarzan's arrows, the latter sat lost in speculation. He seemed continually to be trying to grasp some mental image which as constantly eluded him.

At last he opened the leathern pouch which hung at his side. From it he poured into the palm of his hand a quantity of glittering gems. The firelight playing upon them conjured a multitude of scintillating rays, and as the wide eyes of the Belgian looked on in rapt fascination, the man's expression at last acknowledged a tangible purpose in courting the society of the ape-man.

9

The Theft of the Jewels

FOR two days Werper sought for the party that had accompanied him from the camp to the barrier cliffs; but not until late in the afternoon of the second day did he find clew to its whereabouts, and then in such gruesome form that he was totally unnerved by the sight.

In an open glade he came upon the bodies of three of the

blacks, terribly mutilated, nor did it require considerable deductive power to explain their murder. Of the little party only these three had not been slaves. The others, evidently tempted to hope for freedom from their cruel Arab master, had taken advantage of their separation from the main camp, to slay the three representatives of the hated power which held them in slavery, and vanish into the jungle.

Cold sweat exuded from Werper's forehead as he contemplated the fate which chance had permitted him to escape, for had he been present when the conspiracy bore fruit, he, too, must have been of the garncred.

Tarzan showed not the slightest surprise or interest in the discovery. Inherent in him was a calloused familiarity with violent death. The refinements of his recent civilization expunged by the force of the sad calamity which had befallen him, left only the primitive sensibilities which his childhood's training had imprinted indelibly upon the fabric of his mind.

The training of Kala, the examples and precepts of Kerchak, of Tublat, and of Terkoz now formed the basis of his every thought and action. He retained a mechanical knowledge of French and English speech. Werper had spoken to him in French, and Tarzan had replied in the same tongue without conscious realization that he had departed from the anthropoidal speech in which he had addressed La. Had Werper used English, the result would have been the same.

Again, that night, as the two sat before their camp fire, Tarzan played with his shining baubles. Werper asked him what they were and where he had found them. The ape-man replied that they were gay-colored stones, with which he purposed fashioning a necklace, and that he had found them far beneath the sacrificial court of the temple of the Flaming God.

Werper was relieved to find that Tarzan had no conception of the value of the gems. This would make it easier for the Belgina to obtain possession of them. Possibly the man would give them to him for the asking. Werper reached out his hand toward the little pile that Tarzan had arranged upon a piece of flat wood before him.

"Let me see them," said the Belgian.

Tarzan placed a large palm over his treasure. He bared his fighting fangs, and growled. Werper withdrew his hand more quickly than he had advanced it. Tarzan resumed his playing with the gems, and his conversation with Werper as though nothing unusual had occurred. He had but exhibited the beast's jealous protective instinct for a possession. When he killed he shared the meat with Werper; but had Werper ever, by accident, laid a hand upon Tarzan's share, he would have aroused the same savage, and resentful warning.

From that occurrence dated the beginning of a great fear in the breast of the Belgian for his savage companion. He had never understood the transformation that had been wrought in Tarzan by the blow upon his head, other than to attribute it to a form of amnesia. That Tarzan had once been, in truth, a savage, jungle beast, Werper had not known, and so, of course, he could not guess that the man had reverted to the state in which his childhood and young manhood had been spent.

Now Werper saw in the Englishman a dangerous maniac, whom the slightest untoward accident might turn upon him with rending fangs. Not for a moment did Werper attempt to delude himself into the belief that he could defend himself successfully against an attack by the ape-man. His one hope lay in eluding him, and making for the far distant camp of Achmet Zek as rapidly as he could; but armed only with the sacrificial knife, Werper shrank from attempting the journey through the jungle. Tarzan constituted a protection that was by no means despicable, even in the face of the larger carnivora, as Werper had reason to acknowledge from the evidence he had witnessed in the Oparian temple.

Too, Werper had his covetous soul set upon the pouch of gems, and so he was torn between the various emotions of avarice and fear. But avarice it was that burned most strongly in his breast, to the end that he dared the dangers and suffered the terrors of constant association with him he thought a mad man, rather than give up the hope of obtaining possession of the fortune which the contents of the little pouch represented.

Achmet Zek should know nothing of these—these would be for Werper alone, and so soon as he could encompass his design he would reach the coast and take passage for America, where he could conceal himself beneath the veil of a new identity and enjoy to some measure the fruits of his theft. He had it all planned out, did Lieutenant Albert Werper, living in anticipation the luxurious life of the idle rich. He even found himself regretting that America was so provincial, and that nowhere in the new world was a city that might compare with his beloved Brussels.

It was upon the third day of their progress from Opar that the keen ears of Tarzan caught the sound of men behind them. Werper heard nothing above the humming of the jungle insects, and the chattering life of the lesser monkeys and the birds.

For a time Tarzan stood in statusque silence, listening,

his sensitive nostrils dilating as he assayed each passing breeze. Then he withdrew Werper into the concealment of thick brush, and waited. Presently, along the game trail that Werper and Tarzan had been following, there came in sight a sleek, black warrior, alert and watchful.

In single file behind him, there followed, one after another, near fifty others, each burdened with two dull-yellow ingots lashed upon his back. Werper recognized the party immediately as that which had accompanied Tarzan on his journey to Opar. He glanced at the ape-man; but in the savage, watchful eyes he saw no recognition of Basuli and those other loyal Waziri.

When all had passed, Tarzan rose and emerged from concealment. He looked down the trail in the direction the party had gone. Then he turned to Werper.

"We will follow and slay them," he said.

"Why?" asked the Belgian.

"They are black," explained Tarzan. "It was a black who killed Kala. They are the enemies of the Manganis."

Werper did not relish the idea of engaging in a battle with Basuli and his fierce fighting men. And, again, he had welcomed the sight of them returning toward the Greystoke bungalow, for he had begun to have doubts as to his ability to retrace his steps to the Waziri country. Tarzan, he knew, had not the remotest idea of whither they were going. By keeping at a safe distance behind the laden warriors, they would have no difficulty in following them home. Once at the bungalow, Werper knew the way to the camp of Achmet Zek. There was still another reason why he did not wish to interfere with the Waziri—they were bearing the great burden of treasure in the direction he wished it borne. The farther they took it, the less the distance that he and Achmet Zek would have to transport it.

He argued with the ape-man therefore, against the latter's desire to exterminate the blacks, and at last he prevailed upon Tarzan to follow them in peace, saying that he was sure they would lead them out of the forest into a rich country, teeming with game.

It was many marches from Opar to the Waziri country; but at last came the hour when Tarzan and the Belgian, following the trail of the warriors, topped the last rise, and saw before them the broad Waziri plain, the winding river, and the distant forests to the north and west.

A mile or more ahead of them, the line of warriors was creeping like a giant caterpillar through the tall grasses of the plain. Beyond, grazing herds of zebra, hartebeest, and topi dotted the level landscape, while closer to the river a bull buffalo, his head and shoulders protruding from the reeds watched the advancing blacks for a moment, only to turn at last and disappear into the safety of his dank and gloomy retreat.

Tarzan looked out across the familiar vista with no faintest gleam of recognition in his eyes. He saw the game animals, and his mouth watered; but he did not look in the direction of his bungalow. Werper, however, did. A puzzled expression entered the Belgian's eyes. He shaded them with his palms and gazed long and earnestly toward the spot where the bungalow had stood. He could not credit the testimony of his eyes—there was no bungalow—no barns—no outhouses. The corrals, the hay stacks—all were gone. What could it mean?

And then, slowly there filtered into Werper's consciousness an explanation of the havoc that had been wrought in that peaceful valley since last his eyes had rested upon it—Achmet Zek had been there!

Basuli and his warriors had noted the devastation the moment they had come in sight of the farm. Now they hastened on toward it talking excitedly among themselves in animated speculation upon the cause and meaning of the catastrophe.

When, at last they crossed the trampled garden and stood before the charred ruins of their master's bungalow, their greatest fears became convictions in the light of the evidence about them.

Remnants of human dead, half devoured by prowling hyenas and others of the carnivora which infested the region, lay rotting upon the ground, and among the corpses remained sufficient remnants of their clothing and ornaments to make clear to Basuli the frightful story of the disaster that had befallen his master's house.

"The Arabs," he said, as his men clustered about him.

The Waziri gazed about in mute rage for several minutes. Everywhere they encountered only further evidence of the ruthlessness of the cruel enemy that had come during the Great Bwana's absence and laid waste his property.

"What did they with 'Lady'?" asked one of the blacks.

They had always called Lady Greystoke thus.

"The women they would have taken with them," said Basuli. "Our women and his."

A giant black raised his spear above his head, and gave voice to a savage cry of rage and hate. The others followed his example. Basuli silenced them with a gesture.

"This is no time for useless noises of the mouth," he said. "The Great Bwana has taught us that it is acts by which things are done, not words. Let us save our breath—we shall need it all to follow up the Arabs and slay them. If 'Lady' and our women live the greater the need of haste, and warriors cannot travel fast upon empty lungs."

From the shelter of the reeds along the river, Werper and Tarzan watched the blacks. They saw them dig a trench with their knives and fingers. They saw them lay their yellow burdens in it and scoop the overturned earth back over the tops of the ingots.

Tarzan seemed little interested, after Werper had assured him that that which they buried was not good to eat; but Werper was intensely interested. He would have given much had he had his own followers with him, that he might take away the treasure as soon as the blacks left, for he was sure that they would leave this scene of desolation and death as soon as possible.

The treasure buried, the blacks removed themselves a short distance up wind from the fetid corpses, where they made camp, that they might rest before setting out in pursuit of the Arabs. It was already dusk. Werper and Tarzan sat devouring some pieces of meat they had brought from their last camp. The Belgian was occupied with his plans for the immediate future. He was positive that the Waziri would pursue Achmet Zek, for he knew enough of savage warfare, and of the characteristics of the Arabs and their degraded followers to guess that they had carried the Waziri women off into slavery. This alone would assure immediate pursuit by so warlike a people as the Waziri.

Werper felt that he should find the means and the opportunity to push on ahead, that he might warn Achmet Zek of the coming of Basuli, and also of the location of the buried treasure. What the Arab would now do with Lady Greystoke, in view of the mental affliction of her husband, Werper neither knew nor cared. It was enough that the golden treasure buried upon the site of the burned bungalow was infinitely more valuable than any ransom that would have occurred even to the avaricious mind of the Arab, and if Werper could persuade the raider to share even a portion of it with him he would be well satisfied.

But by far the most important consideration, to Werper, at least, was the incalculably valuable treasure in the little leathern pouch at Tarzan's side. If he could but obtain possession of this! He must! He would!

His eyes wandered to the object of his greed. They measured Tarzan's giant frame, and rested upon the rounded muscles of his arms. It was hopeless. What could he, Werper, hope to accomplish, other than his own death, by an attempt to wrest the gems from their savage owner?

Disconsolate, Werper threw himself upon his side. His

head was pillowed on one arm, the other rested across his face in such a way that his eyes were hidden from the ape-man, though one of them was fastened upon him from beneath the shadow of the Belgian's forearm. For a time he lay thus, glowering at Tarzan, and originating for plundering him of his treasure—schemes that were discarded as futile as rapidly as they were born.

Tarzan presently let his own eyes rest upon Werper. The Belgian saw that he was being watched, and lay very still. After a few moments he simulated the regular breathing of deep slumber.

Tarzan had been thinking. He had seen the Waziri bury their belongings. Werper had told him that they were hiding them lest some one find them and take them away. This seemed to Tarzan a splendid plan for safeguarding valuables. Since Werper had evinced a desire to possess his glittering pebbles. Tarzan, with the suspicions of a savage, had guarded the baubles, of whose worth he was entirely ignorant, as zealously as though they spelled life or death to him.

For a long time the ape-man sat watching his companion. At last, convinced that he slept, Tarzan withdrew his hunting knife and commenced to dig a hole in the ground before him. With the blade he loosened up the earth, and with his hands he scooped it out until he had excavated a little cavity a few inches in diameter, and five or six inches in depth. Into this he placed the pouch of jewels. Werper almost forgot to breathe after the fashion of a sleeper as he saw what the ape-man was doing—he scarce repressed an ejaculation of satisfaction.

Tarzan became suddenly rigid as his keen ears noted the cessation of the regular inspirations and expirations of his companion. His narrowed eyes bored straight down upon the Belgian. Werper felt that he was lost—he must risk all on his ability to carry on the deception. He sighed, threw both arms outward, and turned over on his back mumbling as though in the throes of a bad dream. A moment later he resumed the regular breathing.

Now he could not watch Tarzan, but he was sure that the man sat for a long time looking at him. Then, faintly, Werper heard the other's hands scraping dirt, and later patting it down. He knew then that the jewels were buried.

It was an hour before Werper moved again, then he rolled over facing Tarzan and opened his eyes. The ape-man slept. By reaching out his hand Werper could touch the spot where the pouch was buried.

For a long time he lay watching and listening. He moved about, making more noise than necessary, yet Tarzan did not awaken. He drew the sacrificial knife from his belt, and plunged it into the ground. Tarzan did not move. Cautiously the Belgian pushed the blade downward through the loose earth above the pouch. He felt the point touch the soft, tough fabric of the leather. Then he pried down upon the handle. Slowly the little mound of loose earth rose and parted. An instant later a corner of the pouch came into view. Werper pulled it from its hiding place, and tucked it in his shirt. Then he refilled the hole and pressed the dirt carefully down as it had been before.

Greed had prompted him to an act, the discovery of which by his companion could lead only to the most frightful consequences for Werper. Already he could almost feel those strong, white fangs burying themselves in his neck. He shuddered. Far out across the plain a leopard screamed, and in the dense reeds behind him some great beast moved on padded feet.

Werper feared these prowlers of the night; but infinitely more he feared the just wrath of the human beast sleeping at his side. With utmost caution the Belgian arose. Tarzan did not move. Werper took a few steps toward the plain and the distant forest to the northwest, then he paused and fingered the hilt of the long knife in his belt. He turned and looked down upon the sleeper.

"Why not?" he mused. "Then I should be safe."

He returned and bent above the ape-man. Clutched tightly in his hand was the sacrificial knife of the High Priestess of the Flaming God!

10

Achmet Zek Sees the Jewels

MUGAMBI, weak and suffering, had dragged his painful way along the trail of the retreating raiders. He could move but slowly, resting often; but savage hatred and an equally savage desire for vengeance kept him to his task. As the days passed his wounds healed and his strength returned, until at last his giant frame had regained all of its former mighty powers. Now he went more rapidly; but the mounted Arabs had covered a great distance while the wounded black had been painfully crawling after them.

They had reached their fortified camp, and there Achmet Zek awaited the return of his lieutenant, Albert Werper. During the long, rough journey, Jane Clayton had suffered more in anticipation of her impending fate than from the hardships of the road.

Achmet Zek had not deigned to acquaint her with his intentions regarding her future. She prayed that she had been captured in the hope of ransom, for if such should prove the case, no great harm would befall her at the hands of the Arabs; but there was the chance, the horrid chance, that another fate awaited her. She had heard of many women, among whom were white women, who had been sold by outlaws such as Achmet Zek into the slavery of black harems, or taken farther north into the almost equally hideous existence of some Turkish seraglio.

Jane Clayton was of sterner stuff than that which bends in spineless terror before danger. Until hope proved futile she would not give it up; nor did she entertain thoughts of self-destruction only as a final escape from dishonor. So long as Tarzan lived there was every reason to expect succor. No man nor beast who roamed the savage continent could boast the cunning and the powers of her lord and master. To her, he was little short of omnipotent in his native world —this world of savage beasts and savage men. Tarzan would come, and she should be rescued and avenged, of that she was certain. She counted the days that must elapse before he would return from Opar and discover what had transpired during his absence. After that it would be but a short time before he had surrounded the Arab stronghold and punished the motley crew of wrongdoers who inhabited it.

That he could find her she had no slightest doubt. No spoor, however faint, could elude the keen vigilance of his senses. To him, the trail of the raiders would be as plain as the printed page of an open book to her.

And while she hoped, there came through the dark jungle another. Terrified by night and by day, came Albert Werper. A dozen times he had escaped the claws and fangs of the giant carnivora only by what seemed a miracle to him. Armed with nothing more than the knife he had brought with him from Opar, he had made his way through as savage a country as yet exists upon the face of the globe.

By night he had slept in trees. By day he had stumbled fearfully on, often taking refuge among the branches when sight or sound of some great cat warned him from danger. But at last he had come within sight of the palisade behind which were his fierce companions.

At almost the same time Mugambi came out of the jungle before the walled village. As he stood in the shadow of a great tree, reconnoitering, he saw a man, ragged and disheveled emerge from the jungle almost at his elbow. Instantly he recognized the newcomer as he who had been a guest of his mater before the latter had departed for Opar.

The black was upon the point of hailing the Belgian when something stayed him. He saw the white man walking confidently across the clearing toward the village gate. No sane man thus approached a village in this part of Africa unless he was sure of a friendly welcome. Mugambi waited. His suspicions were aroused.

He heard Werper halloo; he saw the gates swing open, and he witnessed the surprised and friendly welcome that was accorded the erstwhile guest of Lord and Lady Greystoke. A light broke upon the understanding of Mugambi. This white man had been a traitor and a spy. It was to him they owed the raid during the absence of the Great Bwana. To his hate for the Arabs, Mugambi added a still greater hate for the white spy.

Within the village Werper passed hurriedly toward the silken tent of Achmet Zek. The Arab arose as his lieutenant entered. His face showed surprise as he viewed the tattered apparel of the Belgian.

"What has happened?" he asked.

Werper narrated all, save the little matter of the pouch of gems which were now tightly strapped about his waist, beneath his clothing. The Arab's eyes narrowed greedily as his henchman described the treasure that the Waziri had buried beside the ruins of the Greystoke bungalow.

"It will be a simple matter now to return and get it," said Achmet Zek. "First we will await the coming of the rash Waziri, and after we have slain them we may take our time to the treasure—none will disturb it where it lies, for we shall leave none alive who knows of its existence."

"And the woman?" asked Werper.

"I shall sell her in the north," replied the raider. "It is the only way, now. She should bring a good price."

The Belgian nodded. He was thinking rapidly. If he could persuade Achmet Zek to send him in command of the party which took Lady Greystoke north it would give him the opportunity he craved to make his escape from his chief. He would forego a share of the gold, if he could but get away unscathed with the jewels.

He knew Achmet Zek well enough by this time to know that no member of his band ever was voluntarily released from the service of Achmet Zek. Most of the few who deserted were recaptured. More than once had Werper listened to their agonized screams as they were tortured before being put to death. The Belgian had no wish to take the slightest chance of recapture.

"Who will go north with the woman," he asked, "while we are returning for the gold that the Waziri buried by the bungalow of the Englishman?"

Achmet Zek thought for a moment. The buried gold was of much greater value than the price the woman would bring. It was necessary to rid himself of her as quickly as possible and it was also well to obtain the gold with the least possible delay. Of all his followers, the Belgian was the most logical lieutenant to intrust with the command of one of the parties. An Arab, as familiar with the trails and tribes as Achmet Zek himself, might collect the woman's price and make good his escape into the far north. Werper, on the other hand, could scarce make his escape alone through a country hostile to Europeans while the men he would send with the Belgian could be carefully selected with a view to preventing Werper from persuading any considerable portion of his command to accompany him should he contemplate desertion of his chief.

At last the Arab spoke: "It is not necessary that we both return for the gold. You shall go north with the woman, carrying a letter to a friend of mine who is always in touch with the best markets for such merchandise, while I return for the gold. We can meet again here when our business is concluded."

Werper could scarce disguise the joy with which he received this welcome decision. And that he did entirely disguise it from the keen and suspicious eyes of Achmet Zek is open to question. However, the decision reached, the Arab and his lieutenant discussed the details of their forthcoming ventures for a short time further, when Werper made his excuses and returned to his own tent for the comforts and luxury of a long-desired bath and shave.

Having bathed, the Belgian tied a small hand mirror to a cord sewn to the rear wall of his tent, placed a rude chair beside an equally rude table that stood beside the glass, and proceeded to remove the rough stubble from his face.

In the catalog of masculine pleasures there is scarce one which imparts a feeling of greater comfort and refreshment than follows a clean shave, and now, with weariness temporarily banished, Albert Werper sprawled in his rickety chair to enjoy a final cigaret before retiring. His thumbs, tucked in his belt in lazy support of the weight of his arms, touched the belt which held the jewel pouch about his waist. He tingled with excitement as he let his mind dwell upon the value of the treasure, which, unknown to all save himself, lay hid beneath his clothing.

What would Achmet Zek say, if he knew? Werper grinned. How the old rascal's eyes would pop could he but have a glimpse of those scintillating beauties! Werper had never yet had an opportunity to feast his eyes for any great length of time upon them. He had not even counted them—only roughly had he guessed at their value.

He unfastened the belt and drew the pouch from its hiding place. He was alone. The balance of the camp, save the sentries, had retired—none would enter the Belgian's tent. He fingered the pouch, feeling out the shapes and sizes of the precious, little nodules within. He hefted the bag, first in one palm, then in the other, and at last he wheeled his chair slowly around before the table, and in the rays of his small lamp let the glittering gems roll out upon the rough wood.

The refulgent rays transformed the interior of the soiled and squalid canvas to the splendor of a palace in the eyes of the dreaming man. He saw the gilded halls of pleasure that would open their portals to the possessor of the wealth which lay scattered upon this stained and dented table top. He dreamed of joys and luxuries and power which always had been beyond his grasp, and as he dreamed his gaze lifted from the table, as the gaze of a dreamer will, to a far distant goal above the mean horizon of terrestrial commonplaceness.

Unseeing, his eyes rested upon the shaving mirror which still hung upon the tent wall above the table; but his sight was focused far beyond. And then a reflection moved within the polished surface of the tiny glass, the man's eyes shot back out of space to the mirror's face, and in it he saw reflected the grim visage of Achmet Zek, framed in the flaps of the tent doorway behind him.

Werper stifled a gasp of dismay. With rare self-possession he let his gaze drop, without appearing to have halted upon the mirror, until it rested again upon the gems. Without haste, he replaced them in the pouch, tucked the latter into his shirt, selected a cigaret from his case, lighted it and rose. Yawning, and stretching his arms above his head, he turned slowly toward the opposite end of the tent. The face of Achmet Zek had disappeared from the opening.

To say that Albert Werper was terrified would be putting it mildly. He realized that he not only had sacrificed his treasure; but his life as well. Achmet Zek would never permit the wealth that he had discovered to slip through his fingers, nor would he forgive the duplicity of a lieutenant who had gained possession of such a treasure without offering to share it with his chief.

Slowly the Belgian prepared for bed. If he were being watched, he could not know; but if so the watcher saw no indication of the nervous excitement which the European strove to conceal. When ready for his blankets, the man crossed to the little table and extinguished the light.

It was two hours later that the flaps at the front of the tent separated silently and gave entrance to a dark-robed figure, which passed noiselessly from the darkness without to the darkness within. Cautiously the prowler crossed the interior. In one hand was a long knife. He came at last to the pile of blankets spread upon several rugs close to one of the tent walls.

Lightly, his fingers sought and found the bulk beneath the blankets—the bulk that should be Albert Werper. They traced out the figure of a man, and then an arm shot upward, poised for an instant and descended. Again and again it rose and fell, and each time the long blade of the knife buried itself in the thing beneath the blankets. But there was an initial lifelessness in the silent bulk that gave the assassin momentary wonder. Feverishly he threw back the coverlets, and searched with nervous hands for the pouch of jewels which he expected to find concealed upon his victim's body.

An instant later he rose with a curse upon his lips. It was Achmet Zek, and he cursed because he had discovered beneath the blankets of his lieutenant only a pile of discarded clothing arranged in the form and semblance of a sleeping man—Albert Werper had fled.

Out into the village ran the chief, calling in angry tones to the sleepy Arabs, who tumbled from their tents in answer to his voice. But though they searched the village again and again they found no trace of the Belgian. Foaming with anger, Achmet Zek called his followers to horse, and though the night was pitchy black they set out to scour the adjoining forest for their quarry.

As they galloped from the open gates, Mugambi, hiding in a nearby bush, slipped, unseen, within the palisade. A score of blacks crowded about the entrance to watch the searchers depart, and as the last of them passed out of the village the blacks seized the portals and drew them to, and Mugambi lent a hand in the work as though the best of his life had been spent among the raiders.

In the darkness he passed, unchallenged, as one of their number, and as they returned from the gates to their respective tents and huts, Mugambi melted into the shadows and disappeared.

For an hour he crept about in the rear of the various huts and tents in an effort to locate that in which his master's mate was imprisoned. One there was which he was reasonably assured contained her, for it was the only hut before the door of which a sentry had been posted. Mugambi was crouching in the shadow of this structure, just around the corner from the unsuspecting guard, when another approached to relieved his comrade.

"The prisoner is safe within?" asked the newcomer.

"She is," replied the other, "for none has passed this doorway since I came."

The new sentry squatted beside the door, while he whom he had relieved made his way to his own hut. Mugambi slunk closer to the corner of the building. In one powerful hand he gripped a heavy knob-stick. No sign of elation disturbed his phlegmatic calm, yet inwardly he was aroused to joy by the proof he had just heard that "Lady" really was within.

The sentry's back was toward the corner of the hut which hid the giant black. The fellow did not see the huge form which silently loomed behind him. The knob-stick swung upward in a curve, and downward again. There was the sound of a dull thud, the crushing of heavy bone, and the sentry slumped into a silent, inanimate lumb of clay.

A moment later Mugambi was searching the interior of the hut. At first slowly, calling, "Lady!" in a low whisper, and finally with almost frantic haste, until the truth presently dawned upon him—the hut was empty!

11

Tarzan Becomes a Beast Again

FOR a moment Werper had stood above the sleeping apeman, his murderous knife poised for the fatal thrust; but fear stayed his hand. What if the first blow should fail to drive the point to his victim's heart? Werper shuddered in contemplation of the disastrous consequences to himself. Awakened, and even with a few moments of life remaining, the giant could literally tear his assailant to pieces should he choose, and the Belgian had no doubt but that Tarzan would so choose.

Again came the soft sound of padded footsteps in the reeds—closer this time. Werper abandoned his design. Before him stretched the wide plain and escape. The jewels were in his possession. To remain longer was to risk death at the hands of Tarzan, or the jaws of the hunter creeping ever nearer. Turning, he slunk away through the night, toward the distant forest.

Tarzan slept on. Where were those uncanny, guardian powers that had formerly rendered him immune from the dangers of surprise? Could this dull sleeper be the alert, sensitive Tarzan of old?

Perhaps the blow upon his head had numbed his senses, temporarily—who may say? Closer crept the stealthy creature through the reeds. The rustling curtain of vegetation parted a few paces from where the sleeper lay, and the massive head of a lion appeared. The beast surveyed the ape-man intently for a moment, then he crouched, his hind feet drawn well beneath him, his tail lashing from side to side.

It was the beating of the beast's tail against the reeds which awakened Tarzan. Jungle folk do not awaken slowly—instantly, full consciousness and full command of their every faculty returns to them from the depth of profound slumber. Even as Tarzan opened his eyes he was upon his feet, his spear grasped firmly in his hand and ready for attack. Again was he Tarzan of the Apes, sentient, vigilant, ready.

No two lions have identical characteristics, nor does the same lion invariably act similarly under like circumstances. Whether it was surprise, fear or caution which prompted the lion crouching ready to spring upon the man, is immaterial —the fact remains that he did not carry out his original design, he did not spring at the man at all, but, instead, wheeled and sprang back into the reeds as Tarzan arose and confronted him.

The ape-man shrugged his broad shoulders and looked about for his companion. Werper was nowhere to be seen. At first Tarzan suspected that the man had been seized and dragged off by another lion; but upon examination of the ground he soon discovered that the Belgian had gone away alone out into the plain.

For a moment he was puzzled; but presently came to the conclusion that Werper had been frightened by the approach of the lion, and had sneaked off in terror. A sneer touched Tarzan's lips as he pondered the man's act—the desertion of a comrade in time of danger, and without warning. Well, if that was the sort of creature Werper was, Tarzan wished nothing more of him. He had gone, and for all the ape-man cared, he might remain away—Tarzan would not search for him.

A hundred yards from where he stood grew a large tree, alone upon the edge of the reedy jungle. Tarzan made his way to it, clambered into it, and finding a comfortable crotch among its branches, reposed himself for uninterrupted sleep until morning.

And when morning came Tarzan slept on long after the sun had risen. His mind, reverted to the primitive, was untroubled by any more serious obligations than those of providing sustenance, and safeguarding his life. Therefore there was nothing to awaken for until danger threatened, or the pangs of hunger assailed. It was the latter which eventually aroused him.

Opening his eyes, he stretched his giant thews, yawned, rose and gazed about him through the leafy foliage of his retreat. Across the wasted meadowlands and fields of John Clayton, Lord Greystoke, Tarzan of the Apes looked, as a stranger, upon the moving figures of Basuli and his braves as they prepared their morning meal and made ready to set out upon the expedition which Basuli had planned after discovering the havoc and disaster which had befallen the estate of his dead master.

The ape-man eyed the blacks with curiosity. In the back of his brain loitered a fleeting sense of familiarity with all that he saw, yet he could not connect any of the various forms of life, animate and inanimate, which had fallen within the range of his vision since he had emerged from the darkness of the pits of Opar, with any particular event of the past.

Hazily he recalled a grim and hideous form, hairy, ferocious. A vague tenderness dominated his savage sentiments as this phantom memory struggled for recognition. His mind had reverted to his childhood days—it was the figure of the giant she-ape, Kala, that he saw; but only half recognized. He saw, too, other grotesque, manlike forms. They were of Terkoz, Tublat, Kerchak, and a smaller, less ferocious figure, that was Neeta, the little playmate of his boyhood.

Slowly, very slowly, as these visions of the past animated his lethargic memory, he came to recognize them. They took definite shape and form, adjusting themselves nicely to the various incidents of his life with which they had been intimately connected. His boyhood among the apes spread itself in a slow panorama before him, and as it unfolded it induced within him a mighty longing for the companionship of the shaggy, low-browed brutes of his past.

He watched the blacks scatter their cook fire and depart; but though the face of each of them had but recently been as familiar to him as his own, they awakened within him no recollections whatsoever.

When they had gone, he descended from the tree and sought food. Out upon the plain grazed numerous herds of wild ruminants. Toward a sleek, fat bunch of zebra he wormed his stealthy way. No intricate process of reasoning caused him to circle widely until he was down wind from his prey—he acted instinctively. He took advantage of every form of cover as he crawled upon all fours and often flat upon his stomach toward them.

A plump young mare and a fat stallion grazed nearest to him as he neared the herd. Again it was instinct which selected the former for his meat. A low bush grew but a few yards from the unsuspecting two. The ape-man reached its shelter. He gathered his spear firmly in his grasp. Cautiously he drew his feet beneath him. In a single swift move he rose and cast his heavy weapon at the mare's side. Nor did he wait to note the effect of his assault, but leaped cat-like after his spear, his hunting knife in his hand.

For an instant the two animals stood motionless. The tearing of the cruel barb into her side brought a sudden scream of pain and fright from the mare, and then they both wheeled and broke for safety; but Tarzan of the Apes, for a distance of a few yards, could equal the speed of even these, and the first stride of the mare found her overhauled, with a savage beast at her shoulder. She turned, biting and kicking at her foe. Her mate hesitated for an instant, as though about to rush to her assistance; but a backward glance revealed to him the flying heels of the balance of the herd, and with a snort and a shake of his head he wheeled and dashed away.

Clinging with one hand to the short mane of his quarry, Tarzan struck again and again with his knife at the unprotected heart. The result had, from the first, been inevitable. The mare fought bravely, but hopelessly, and presently sank to the earth, her heart pierced. The ape-man placed a foot upon her carcass and raised his voice in the victory call of the Mangani. In the distance, Basuli halted as the faint notes of the hideous scream broke upon his ears.

"The great apes," he said to his companion. "It has been long since I have heard them in the country of the Waziri. What could have brought them back?"

Tarzan grasped his kill and dragged it to the partial seclusion of the bush which had hidden his own near approach, and there he squatted upon it, cut a huge hunk of flesh from the loin and proceeded to satisfy his hunger with the warm and dripping meat.

Attracted by the shrill screams of the mare, a pair of hyenas slunk presently into view. They trotted to a point a few yards from the gorging ape-man, and halted. Tarzan looked up, bared his fightings fangs and growled. The hyenas returned the compliment, and withdrew a couple of paces. They made no move to attack; but continued to sit at a respectful distance until Tarzan had concluded his meal. After the ape-man had cut a few strips from the carcass to carry with him, he walked slowly off in the direction of the river to quench his thirst. His way lay directly toward the hyenas, nor did he alter his course because of them.

With all the lordly majesty of Numa, the lion, he strode straight toward the growling beasts. For a moment they held their ground, bristling and defiant; but only for a moment, and then slunk away to one side while the indifferent ape-man passed them on his lordly way. A moment later they were tearing at the remains of the zebra.

Back to the reeds went Tarzan, and through them toward the river. A heard of buffalo, startled by his approach, rose ready to charge or to fly. A great bull pawed the ground and bellowed as his bloodshot eyes discovered the intruder; but the ape-man passed across their front as though ignorant of their existence. The bull's bellowing lessened to a low rumbling, he turned and scraped a horde of flies from his side with his muzzle, cast a final glance at the ape-man and resumed his feeding. His numerous family either followed his example or stood gazing after Tarzan in mild-eyed curiosity, until the opposite reeds swallowed him from view.

At the river, Tarzan drank his fill and bathed. During the heat of the day he lay up under the shade of a tree near the ruins of his burned barns. His eyes wandered out across the plain toward the forest, and a longing for the pleasures of its mysterious depths possessed his thoughts for a considerable time. With the next sun he would cross the open and enter the forest! There was no hurry—there lay before him an endless vista of tomorrows with naught to fill them but the satisfying of the appetites and caprices of the moment.

The ape-man's mind was untroubled by regret for the past, or aspiration for the future. He could lie at full length along a swaying branch, stretching his giant limbs, and luxuriating in the blessed peace of utter thoughtlessness, without an apprehension or a worry to sap his nervous energy and rob him of his peace of mind. Recalling only dimly any other existence, the ape-man was happy. Lord Greystoke had ceased to exist.

For several hours Tarzan lolled upon his swaying, leafy couch until once again hunger and thirst suggested an excursion. Stretching lazily he dropped to the ground and moved slowly toward the river. The game trail down which he walked had become by ages of use a deep, narrow trench, its walls topped on either side by impenetrable thicket and dense-growing trees closely interwoven with thick-stemmed creepers and lesser vines inextricably matted into two solid ramparts of vegetation. Tarzan had almost reached the point where the trail debouched upon the open river bottom when he saw a family of lions approaching along the path from the direction of the river. The ape-man counted seven—a male and two lionesses, full grown, and four young lions as large and quite as formidable as their parents. Tarzan halted, growling, and the lions paused, the great male in the lead baring his fangs and rumbling forth a warning roar. In his hand the ape-man held his heavy spear; but he had no intention of pitting his puny weapon against seven lions; yet he stood there growling and roaring and the lions did likewise. It was purely an exhibition of jungle bluff. Each was trying to frighten off the other. Neither wished to turn back and give way, nor did either at first desire to precipitate an encounter. The lions were fed up sufficiently so as not to be goaded by pangs of hunger and as for Tarzan he seldom ate the meat of the carnivores; but a point of ethics was at stake and neither side wished to back down. So they stood there facing one another, making all sorts of hideous noises the while they hurled jungle invective back and forth. How long this bloodless duel would have persisted it is difficult to say, though eventually Tarzan would have been forced to yield to superior numbers.

There came, however, an interruption which put an end to the deadlock and it came from Tarzan's rear. He and the lions had been making so much noise that neither could hear anything above their concerted bedlam, and so it was that Tarzan did not hear the great bulk bearing down upon him from behind until an instant before it was upon him, and then he turned to see Buto, the rhinoceros, his little, pig eyes blazing, charging madly toward him and already so close that escape seemed impossible; yet so perfectly were mind and muscles coördinated in this unspoiled, primitive man that almost simultaneously with the sense perception of the threatened danger he wheeled and hurled his spear at Buto's chest. It was a heavy spear shod with iron, and behind it were the giant muscles of the ape-man, while coming to meet it was the enormous weight of Buto and the momentum of his rapid rush. All that happened in the instant that Tarzan turned to meet the charge of the irascible rhinoceros might take long to tell, and yet would have taxed the swiftest lens to record. As his spear left his hand the ape-man was looking down upon the mighty horn lowered to toss him, so close was Buto to him. The spear entered the rhinoceros' neck at its junction with the left shoulder and passed almost entirely through the beast's body, and at the instant that he launched it, Tarzan leaped straight into the air alighting upon Buto's back but escaping the mighty horn.

Then Buto espied the lions and bore madly down upon them while Tarzan of the Apes leaped nimbly into the tangled creepers at one side of the trail. The first lion met Buto's charge and was tossed high over the back of the maddened brute, torn and dying, and then the six remaining lions were upon the rhinoceros, rending and tearing the while they were being gored or trampled. From the safety of his perch Tarzan watched the battle royal with the keenest interest, for the more intelligent of the jungle folk are interested in such encounters. They are to them what the race track and the prize ring, the theater and the movies are to us. They see them often; but always they enjoy them for no two are precisely alike.

For a time it seemed to Tarzan that Buto, the rhinoceros, would prove victor in the gory battle. Already had he accounted for four of the seven lions and badly wounded the three remaining when in a momentary lull in the encounter he sank limply to his knees and rolled over upon his side. Tarzan's spear had done its work. It was the man-made weapon which killed the great beast that might easily have survived the assault of seven mighty lions, for Tarzan's spear had pierced the great lungs, and Buto, with victory almost in sight, succumbed to internal hemorrhage.

Then Tarzan came down from his sanctuary and as the wounded lions, growling, dragged themselves away, the ape-man cut his spear from the body of Buto, hacked off a steak and vanished into the jungle. The episode was over. It had been all in the day's work—something which you and I might talk about for a lifetime Tarzan dismissed from his mind the moment that the scene passed from his sight.

12

La Seeks Vengeance

Swinging back through the jungle in a wide circle the ape-man came to the river at another point, drank and took to the trees again and while he hunted, all oblivious of his past and careless of his future, there came through the dark jungles and the open, parklike places and across the wide meadows, where grazed the countless herbivora of the mysterious continent, a weird and terrible caravan in search of him. There were fifty frightful men with hairy bodies and gnarled and crooked legs. They were armed with knives and great bludgeons and at their head marched an almost naked woman, beautiful beyond compare. It was La of Opar, High Priestess of the Flaming God, and fifty of her horrid priests searching for the purloiner of the sacred sacrificial knife.

Never before had La passed beyond the crumbling outer walls of Opar; but never before had need been so insistent. The sacred knife was gone! Handed down through countless ages it had come to her as a heritage and an insignia of her religious office and regal authority from some long-dead progenitor of lost and forgotten Atlantis. The loss of the crown jewels or the Great Seal of England could have brought no greater consternation to a British king than did the pilfering of the sacred knife bring to La, the Oparian, Queen and High Priestess of the degraded remnants of the oldest civilization upon earth. When Atlantis, with all her mighty cities and her cultivated fields and her great commerce and culture and riches sank into the sea long ages since, she took with her all but a handful of her colonists working the vast gold mines of Central Africa. From these and their degraded slaves and a later intermixture of the blood of the anthropoids sprung the gnarled men of Opar; but by some queer freak of fate, aided by natural selection, the old Atlantean strain had remained pure and undegraded in the females descended from a single princess of the royal house of Atlantis who had been in Opar at the time of the great catastrophe. Such was La.

Burning with white-hot anger was the High Priestess, her heart a seething, molten mass of hatred for Tarzan of the Apes. The zeal of the religious fanatic whose altar has been desecrated was triply enhanced by the rage of a woman scorned. Twice had she thrown her heart at the feet of the godlike ape-man and twice had she been repulsed. La knew that she was beautiful—and she was beautiful, not by the standards of prehistoric Atlantis alone, but by those of modern times was La physically a creature of perfection. Before Tarzan came that first time to Opar, La had never seen a human male other than the grotesque and knotted men of her clan. With one of these she must mate sooner or later that the direct line of high priestesses might not be broken, unless Fate should bring other men to Opar. Before Tarzan came upon his first visit, La had had no thought that such men as he existed, for she knew only her hideous little priests and the bulls of the tribe of great anthropoids that had dwelt from time immemorial in and about Opar, until they had come to be looked upon almost as equals by the Oparians. Among the legends of Opar were tales of godlike men of the olden time and of black men who had come more recently; but these latter had been enemies who killed and robbed. And, too, these legends always held forth the hope that some day that nameless continent from which their race had sprung, would rise once more out of the sea and with slaves at the long sweeps would send her carven, gold-picked galleys forth to succor the long-exiled colonists.

The coming of Tarzan had aroused within La's breast the wild hope that at last the fulfillment of this ancient prophecy was at hand; but more strongly still had it aroused the hot fires of love in a heart that never otherwise would have known the meaning of that all-consuming passion, for such a wondrous creature as La could never have felt love for any of the repulsive priests of Opar. Custom, duty and religious zeal might have commanded the union; but there could have been no love on La's part. She had grown to young womanhood a cold and heartless creature, daughter of a thousand other cold, heartless, beautiful women who had never known love. And so when love came to her it liberated all the pent passions of a thousand generations, transforming La into a pulsing, throbbing volcano of desire, and with desire thwarted this great force of love and gentleness and sacrifice was transmuted by its own fires into one of hatred and revenge.

It was in a state of mind superinduced by these conditions that La led forth her jabbering company to retrieve the sacred emblem of her high office and wreak vengeance upon the author of her wrongs. To Werper she gave little thought. The fact that the knife had been in his hand when it departed from Opar brought down no thoughts of vengeance upon his head. Of course, he should be slain when captured;

but his death would give La no pleasure—she looked for that in the contemplated death agonies of Tarzan. He should be tortured. His should be a slow and frightful death. His punishment should be adequate to the immensity of his crime. He had wrested the sacred knife from La; he had lain sacrilegious hands upon the High Priestess of the Flaming God; he had desecrated the altar and the temple. For these things he should die; but he had scorned the love of La, the woman, and for this he should die horribly with great anguish.

The march of La and her priests was not without its adventures. Unused were these to the ways of the jungle, since seldom did any venture forth from behind Opar's crumbling walls, yet their very numbers protected them and so they came without fatalities far along the trail of Tarzan and Werper. Three great apes accompanied them and to these was delegated the business of tracking the quarry, a feat beyond the senses of the Oparians. La commanded. She arranged the order of march, she selected the camps, she set the hour for halting and the hour for resuming and though she was inexperienced in such matters, her native intelligence was so far above that of the men or the apes that she did better than they could have done. She was a hard taskmaster, too, for she looked down with loathing and contempt upon the misshapen creatures amongst which cruel Fate had thrown her and to some extent vented upon them. her dissatisfaction and her thwarted love. She made them build her a strong protection and shelter each night and keep a great fire burning before it from dusk to dawn. When she tired of walking they were forced to carry her upon an improvised litter, nor did one dare to question her authority or her right to such services. In fact they did not question either. To them she was a goddess and each loved her and each hoped that he would be chosen as her mate, so they. slaved for her and bore the stinging lash of her displeasure and the habitually haughty disdain of her manner without a murmur.

For many days they marched, the apes following the trail easily and going a little distance ahead of the body of the caravan that they might warn the others of impending danger. It was during a noonday halt while all were lying resting after a tiresome march that one of the apes rose suddenly and sniffed the breeze. In a low guttural he cautioned the others to silence and a moment later was swinging quietly up wind into the jungle. La and the priests gathered silently together, the hideous little men fingering their knives and bludgeons, and awaited the return of the shaggy anthropoid.

Nor had they long to wait before they saw him emerge

from a leafy thicket and approach them. Straight to La he came and in the language of the great apes which was also the language of decadent Opar he addressed her.

"The great Tarmangani lies asleep there," he said, pointing in the direction from which he had just come. "Come and we can kill him."

"Do not kill him," commanded La in cold tones. "Bring the great Tarmangani to me alive and unhurt. The vengeance is La's. Go; but make no sound!" and she waved her hands to include all her followers.

Cautiously the weird party crept through the jungle in the wake of the great ape until at last he halted them with a raised hand and pointed upward and a little ahead. There they saw the giant form of the ape-man stretched along a low bough and even in sleep one hand grasped a stout limb and one strong, brown leg reached out and overlapped another. At ease lay Tarzan of the Apes, sleeping heavily upon a full stomach and dreaming of Numa, the lion, and Horta, the boar, and other creatures of the jungle. No intimation of danger assailed the dormant faculties of the ape-man—he saw no crouching hairy figures upon the ground beneath him nor the three apes that swung quietly into the tree beside him.

The first intimation of danger that came to Tarzan was the impact of three bodies as the three apes leaped upon him and hurled him to the ground, where he alighted half stunned beneath their combined weight and was immediately set upon by the fifty hairy men or as many of them as could swarm upon his person. Instantly the ape-man became the center of a whirling, striking, biting maelstrom of horror. He fought nobly but the odds against him were too great. Slowly they overcame him though there was scarce one of them that did not feel the weight of his mighty fist or the rending of his fangs.

13

Condemned To Torture and Death

LA HAD followed her company and when she saw them clawing and biting at Tarzan, she raised her voice and cautioned them not to kill him. She saw that he was weakening and that soon the greater numbers would prevail over him, nor had she long to wait before the mighty jungle creature lay helpless and bound at her feet.

"Bring him to the place at which we stopped," she commanded and they carried Tarzan back to the little clearing and threw him down beneath a tree.

"Build me a shelter!" ordered La. "We shall stop here tonight and tomorrow in the face of the Flaming God, La will offer up the heart of this defiler of the temple. Where is the sacred knife? Who took it from him?"

But no one had seen it and each was positive in his assurance that the sacrificial weapon had not been upon Tarzan's person when they captured him. The ape-man looked upon the menacing creatures which surrounded him and snarled his defiance. He looked upon La and smiled. In the face of death he was unafraid.

"Where is the knife?" La asked him.

"I do not know," replied Tarzan. "The man took it with him when he slipped away during the night. Since you are so desirous for its return I would look for him and get it back for you, did you not hold me prisoner; but now that I am to die I cannot get it back. Of what good was your knife, anyway? You can make another. Did you follow us all this way for nothing more than a knife? Let me go and find him and I will bring it back to you."

La laughed a bitter laugh, for in her heart she knew that Tarzan's sin was greater than the purloining of the sacrificial knife of Opar; yet as she looked at him lying bound and helpless before her, tears rose to her eyes so that she had to turn away to hide them; but she remained inflexible in her determination to make him pay in frightful suffering and in eventual death for daring to spurn the love of La.

When the shelter was completed La had Tarzan transferred to it. "All night I shall torture him," she muttered to her priests, "and at the first streak of dawn you may prepare the flaming altar upon which his heart shall be offered up to the Flaming God. Gather wood well filled with pitch, lay it in the form and size of the altar at Opar in the center of the clearing that the Flaming God may look down upon our handiwork and be pleased."

During the balance of the day the priests of Opar were busy erecting an altar in the center of the clearing, and while they worked they chanted weird hymns in the ancient tongue of that lost continent that lies at the bottom of the Atlantic. They knew not the meanings of the words they mouthed; they but repeated the ritual that had been handed down from preceptor to neophyte since that long-gone day when the ancestors of the Piltdown man still swung by their tails in the humid jungles that are England now.

And in the shelter of the hut, La paced to and fro beside the stoic ape-man. Resigned to his fate was Tarzan. No hope of succor gleamed through the dead black of the death sentence hanging over him. He knew that his giant muscles could not part the many strands that bound his wrists and ankles, for he had strained often, but ineffectually for release. He had no hope of outside help and only enemies surrounded him within the camp, and yet he smiled at La as she paced nervously back and forth the length of the shelter.

And La? She fingered her knife and looked down upon her captive. She glared and muttered but she did not strike. "Tonight!" she thought. "Tonight, when it is dark I will torture him." She looked upon his perfect, godlike figure and upon his handsome, smiling face and then she steeled her heart again by thoughts of her love spurned; by religious thoughts that damned the infidel who had desecrated the holy of holies; who had taken from the blood-stained altar of Opar the offering to the Flaming God—and not once but thrice. Three times had Tarzan cheated the god of her fathers. At the thought La paused and knelt at his side. In her hand was a sharp knife. She placed its point against the ape-man's side and pressed upon the hilt; but Tarzan only smiled and shrugged his shoulders.

How beautiful he was! La bent low over him, looking into his eyes. How perfect was his figure. She compared it with those of the knurled and knotted men from whom she must choose a mate, and La shuddered at the thought. Dusk came and after dusk came night. A great fire blazed within the little thorn boma about the camp. The flames played upon the new altar erected in the center of the clearing, arousing in the mind of the High Priestess of the Flaming God a picture of the event of the coming dawn. She saw this giant and perfect form writhing amid the flames of the burning pyre. She saw those smiling lips, burned and blackened, falling away from the strong, white teeth. She saw the shock of black hair tousled upon Tarzan's well-shaped head disappear in a spurt of flame. She saw these and many other frightful pictures as she stood with closed eyes and clenched fists above the object of her hate—ah! was it hate that La of Opar felt?

The darkness of the jungle night had settled down upon the camp, relieved only by the fitful flarings of the fire that was kept up to warn off the man-eaters. Tarzan lay quietly in his bonds. He suffered from thirst and from the cutting of the tight strands about his wrists and ankles; but he made no complaint. A jungle beast was Tarzan with the stoicism of the beast and the intelligence of man. He knew that his doom was sealed—that no supplications would avail to temper the severity of his end and so he wasted no breath in pleadings; but waited patiently in the firm conviction that his sufferings could not endure forever.

In the darkness La stooped above him. In her hand was a sharp knife and in her mind the determination to initiate his torture without further delay. The knife was pressed against his side and La's face was close to his when a sudden burst of flame from new branches thrown upon the fire without, lighted up the interior of the shelter. Close beneath her lips La saw the perfect features of the forest god and into her woman's heart welled all the great love she had felt for Tarzan since first she had seen him, and all the accumulated passion of the years that she had dreamed of him.

Dagger in hand, La, the High Priestess, towered above the helpless creature that had dared to violate the sanctuary of her deity. There should be no torture—there should be instant death. No longer should the defiler of the temple pollute the sight of the lord god almighty. A single stroke of the heavy blade and then the corpse to the flaming pyre without. The knife arm stiffened ready for the downward plunge, and then La, the woman, collapsed weakly upon the body of the man she loved.

She ran her hands in mute caress over his naked flesh; she covered his forehead, his eyes, his lips with hot kisses; she covered him with her body as though to protect him from the hideous fate she had ordained for him, and in trembling, piteous tones she begged him for his love. For hours the frenzy of her passion possessed the burning handmaiden of the Flaming God, until at last sleep overpowered her and she lapsed into unconsciousness beside the man she had sworn to torture and to slay. And Tarzan, untroubled by thoughts of the future, slept peacefully in La's embrace.

At the first hint of dawn the chanting of the priests of Opar brought Tarzan to wakefulness. Initiated in low and subdued tones, the sound soon rose in volume to the open diapason of barbaric blood lust. La stirred. Her perfect arm pressed Tarzan closer to her—a smile parted her lips and then she awoke, and slowly the smile faded and her eyes went wide in horror as the significance of the death chant impinged upon her understanding.

"Love me, Tarzan!" she cried. "Love me, and you shall be saved."

Tarzan's bonds hurt him. He was suffering the tortures of long-restricted circulation. With an angry growl he rolled over with his back toward La. That was her answer! The High Priestess leaped to her feet. A hot flush of shame mantled her cheek and then she went dead white and stepped to the shelter's entrance.

"Come, Priests of the Flaming God!" she cried, "and make ready the sacrifice."

The warped things advanced and entered the shelter. They laid hands upon Tarzan and bore him forth, and as they chanted they kept time with their crooked bodies, swaying to and fro to the rhythm of their song of blood and death. Behind them came La, swaying too; but not in unison with the chanted cadence. White and drawn was the face of the High Priestess—white and drawn with unrequited love and hideous terror of the moments to come. Yet stern in her resolve was La. The infidel should die! The scorner of her love should pay the price upon the fiery altar. She saw them lay the perfect body there upon the rough branches. She saw the High Priest, he to whom custom would unite her— bent, crooked, gnarled, stunted, hideous—advance with the flaming torch and stand awaiting her command to apply it to the faggots surrounding the sacrificial pyre. His hairy, bestial face was distorted in a yellow-fanged grin of anticipatory enjoyment. His hands were cupped to receive the life blood of the victim—the red nectar that at Opar would have filled the golden sacrificial goblets.

La approached with upraised knife, her face turned toward the rising sun and upon her lips a prayer to the burning deity of her people. The High Priest looked questioningly toward her—the brand was burning close to his hand and the faggots lay temptingly near. Tarzan closed his eyes and awaited the end. He knew that he would suffer, for he recalled the faint memories of past burns. He knew that he would suffer and die; but he did not flinch. Death is no great adventure to the jungle bred who walk hand-in-hand with the grim specter by day and lie down at his side by night through all the years of their lives. It is doubtful that the ape-man even speculated upon what came after death. As a matter of fact as his end approached, his mind was occupied by thoughts of the pretty pebbles he had lost, yet his every faculty still was open to what passed around him.

He felt La lean over him and he opened his eyes. He saw her white, drawn face and he saw tears blinding her eyes. "Tarzan, my Tarzan!" she moaned, "tell me that you love me—that you will return to Opar with me—and you shall live. Even in the face of the anger of my people I will save you. This last chance I give you. What is your answer?"

At the last moment the woman in La had triumphed over

the High Priestess of a cruel cult. She saw upon the altar the only creature that ever had aroused the fires of love within her virgin breast; she saw the beast-faced fanatic who would one day be her mate, unless she found another less repulsive, standing with the burning torch ready to ignite the pyre; yet with all her mad passion for the ape-man she would give the word to apply the flame if Tarzan's final answer was unsatisfactory. With heaving bosom she leaned close above him. "Yes or no?" she whispered.

Through the jungle, out of the distance, came faintly a sound that brought a sudden light of hope to Tarzan's eyes. He raised his voice in a weird scream that sent La back from him a step or two. The impatient priest grumbled and switched the torch from one hand to the other at the same time holding it closer to the tinder at the base of the pyre.

"Your answer!" insisted La. "What is your answer to the love of La of Opar?"

Closer came the sound that had attracted Tarzan's attention and now the others heard it—the shrill trumpeting of an elephant. As La looked wide-eyed into Tarzan's face, there to read her fate for happiness or heartbreak, she saw an expression of concern shadow his features. Now, for the first time, she guessed the meaning of Tarzan's shrill scream—he had summoned Tantor, the elephant, to his rescue! La's brows contracted in a savage scowl. "You refuse La!" she cried. "Then die! The torch!" she commanded, turning toward the priest.

Tarzan looked up into her face. "Tantor is coming," he said. "I thought that he would rescue me; but I know now from his voice that he will slay me and you and all that fall in his path, searching out with the cunning of Sheeta, the panther, those who would hide from him, for Tantor is mad with the madness of love."

La knew only too well the insane ferocity of a bull elephant in *must*. She knew that Tarzan had not exaggerated. She knew that the devil in the cunning, cruel brain of the great beast might send it hither and thither hunting through the forest for those who escaped its first charge, or the beast might pass on without returning—no one might guess which.

"I cannot love you, La," said Tarzan in a low voice. "I do not know why, for you are very beautiful. I could not go back and live in Opar—I who have the whole broad jungle for my range. No, I cannot love you but I cannot see you die beneath the goring tusks of mad Tantor. Cut my bonds before it is too late. Already he is almost upon us. Cut them and I may yet save you."

A little spiral of curling smoke rose from one corner of the pyre—the flames licked upward, crackling. La stood there like a beautiful statue of despair gazing at Tarzan and at the spreading flames. In a moment they would reach out and grasp him. From the tangled forest came the sound of cracking limbs and crashing trunks—Tantor was coming down upon them, a huge Juggernaut of the jungle. The priests were becoming uneasy. They cast apprehensive glances in the direction of the approaching elephant and then back at La.

"Fly!" she commanded them and then she stooped and cut the bonds securing her prisoner's feet and hands. In an instant Tarzan was upon the ground. The priests screamed out their rage and disappointment. He with the torch took a menacing step toward La and the ape-man. "Traitor!" he shrieked at the woman. "For this you too shall die!" Raising his bludgeon he rushed upon the High Priestess; but Tarzan was there before her. Leaping in to close quarters the ape-man seized the upraised weapon and wrenched it from the hands of the frenzied fanatic and then the priest closed upon him with tooth and nail. Seizing the stocky, stunted body in his mighty hands Tarzan raised the creature high above his head, hurling him at his fellows who were now gathered ready to bear down upon their erstwhile captive. La stood proudly with ready knife behind the ape-man. No faint sign of fear marked her perfect brow—only haughty disdain for her priests and admiration for the man she loved so hopelessly filled her thoughts.

Suddenly upon this scene burst the mad bull—a huge tusker, his little eyes inflamed with insane rage. The priests stood for an instant paralyzed with terror; but Tarzan turned and gathering La in his arms raced for the nearest tree. Tantor bore down upon him trumpeting shrilly. La clung with both white arms about the ape-man's neck. She felt him leap into the air and marveled at his strength and his agility as, burdened with her weight, he swung nimbly into the lower branches of a large tree and quickly bore her upward beyond reach of the sinuous trunk of the pachyderm.

Momentarily baffled here, the huge elephant wheeled and bore down upon the hapless priests who had now scattered, terror-stricken, in every direction. The nearest he gored and threw high among the branches of a tree. One he seized in the coils of his trunk and broke upon a huge bole, dropping the mangled pulp to charge, trumpeting, after another. Two he trampled beneath his huge feet and by then the others had disappeared into the jungle. Now Tantor turned his attention once more to Tarzan for one of the symptoms of madness is a revulsion of affection—objects of sane love become the objects of insane hatred. Peculiar in the unwritten annals of the jungle was the proverbial love that had existed between the ape-man and the tribe of Tantor. No elephant in all the jungle would harm the Tarmangani—the white-ape; but with the madness of *must* upon him the great bull sought to destroy his long-time play-fellow.

Back to the tree where La and Tarzan perched came Tantor, the elephant. He reared up with his forefeet against the bole and reached high toward them with his long trunk; but Tarzan had foreseen this and clambered beyond the bull's longest reach. Failure but tended to further enrage the mad creature. He bellowed and trumpeted and screamed until the earth shook to the mighty volume of his noise. He put his head against the tree and pushed and the tree bent before his mighty strength; yet still it held.

The actions of Tarzan were peculiar in the extreme. Had Numa, or Sabor, or Sheeta, or any other beast of the jungle been seeking to destroy him, the ape-man would have danced about hurling missiles and invective at his assailant. He would have insulted and taunted them, reviling in the jungle Billingsgate he knew so well; but now he sat silent out of Tantor's reach and upon his handsome face was an expression of deep sorrow and pity, for of all the jungle folk Tarzan loved Tantor the best. Could he have slain him he would not have thought of doing so. His one idea was to escape, for he knew that with the passing of the *must* Tantor would be sane again and that once more he might stretch at full length upon that mighty back and make foolish speech into those great, flapping ears.

Finding that the tree would not fall to his pushing, Tantor was but enraged the more. He looked up at the two perched high above him, his red-rimmed eyes blazing with insane hatred, and then he wound his trunk about the bole of the tree, spread his great feet wide apart and tugged to uproot the jungle giant. A huge creature was Tantor, an enormous bull in the full prime of all his stupendous strength. Mightily he strove until presently, to Tarzan's consternation, the great tree gave slowly at the roots. The ground rose in little mounds and ridges about the base of the bole, the tree tilted—in another moment it would be uprooted and fall.

The ape-man whirled La to his back and just as the tree inclined slowly in its first movement out of the perpendicular, before the sudden rush of its final collapse, he swung to the branches of a lesser neighbor. It was a long and perilous leap. La closed her eyes and shuddered; but when she opened them again she found herself safe and Tarzan whirling onward through the forest. Behind them the uprooted tree crashed heavily to the ground, carrying with it the lesser trees in its path and then Tantor, realizing that his prey had escaped him, set up once more his hideous trumpeting and followed at a rapid charge upon their trail.

14

A Priestess But Yet a Woman

AT FIRST La closed her eyes and clung to Tarzan in terror, though she made no outcry; but presently she gained sufficient courage to look about her, to look down at the ground beneath and even to keep her eyes open during the wide, perilous swings from tree to tree, and then there came over her a sense of safety because of her confidence in the perfect physical creature in whose strength and nerve and agility her fate lay. Once she raised her eyes to the burning sun and murmured a prayer of thanks to her pagan god that she had not been permitted to destroy this godlike man, and her long lashes were wet with tears. A strange anomaly was La of Opar—a creature of circumstance torn by conflicting emotions. Now the cruel and bloodthirsty creature of a heartless god and again a melting woman filled with compassion and tenderness. Sometimes the incarnation of jealousy and revenge and sometimes a sobbing maiden, generous and forgiving; at once a virgin and a wanton; but always—a woman. Such was La.

She pressed her cheek close to Tarzan's shoulder. Slowly she turned her head until her hot lips were pressed again his flesh. She loved him and would gladly have died for him; yet within an hour she had been ready to plunge a knife into his heart and might again within the coming hour.

A hapless priest seeking shelter in the jungle chanced to show himself to enraged Tantor. The great beast turned to one side, bore down upon the crooked, little man, snuffed him out and then, diverted from his course, blundered away toward the south. In a few minutes even the noise of his trumpeting was lost in the distance.

Tarzan dropped to the ground and La slipped to her feet from his back. "Call your people together," said Tarzan.

"They will kill me," replied La.

"They will not kill you," contradicted the ape-man. "No

one will kill you while Tarzan of the Apes is here. Call them and we will talk with them."

La raised her voice in a weird, flutelike call that carried far into the jungle on every side. From near and far came answering shouts in the barking tones of the Oparian priests: "We come! We come!" Again and again, La repeated her summons until singly and in pairs the greater portion of her following approached and halted a short distance away from the High Priestess and her savior. They came with scowling brows and threatening mien. When all had come Tarzan addressed them.

"Your La is safe," said the ape-man. "Had she slain me she would now herself be dead and many more of you; but she spared me that I might save her. Go your way with her back to Opar, and Tarzan will go his way into the jungle. Let there be peace always between Tarzan and La. What is your answer?"

The priests grumbled and shook their heads. They spoke together and La and Tarzan could see that they were not favorably inclined toward the proposition. They did not wish to take La back and they did wish to complete the sacrifice of Tarzan to the Flaming God. At last the ape-man became impatient.

"You will obey the commands of your queen," he said, "and go back to Opar with her or Tarzan of the Apes will call together the other creatures of the jungle and slay you all. La saved me that I might save you and her. I have served you better alive than I could have dead. If you are not all fools you will let me go my way in peace and you will return to Opar with La. I know not where the sacred knife is; but you can fashion another. Had I not taken it from La you would have slain me and now your god must be glad that I took it since I have saved his priestess from love-mad Tantor. Will you go back to Opar with La, promising that no harm shall befall her?"

The priests gathered together in a little knot arguing and discussing. They pounded upon their breasts with their fists; they raised their hands and eyes to their fiery god; they growled and barked among themselves until it became evident to Tarzan that one of their number was preventing the acceptance of his proposal. This was the High Priest whose heart was filled with jealous rage because La openly acknowledged her love for the stranger, when by the world customs of their cult she should have belonged to him. Seemingly there was to be no solution of the problem until another priest stepped forth and, raising his hand, addressed La.

"Cadj, the High Priest," he announced, "would sacrifice you both to the Flaming God; but all of us except Cadj would gladly return to Opar with our queen."

"You are many against one," spoke up Tarzan. "Why should you not have your will? Go your way with La to Opar and if Cadj interferes slay him."

The priests of Opar welcomed this suggestion with loud cries of approval. To them it appeared nothing short of divine inspiration. The influence of ages of unquestioning obedience to high priests had made it seem impossible to them to question his authority; but when they realized that they could force him to their will they were as happy as children with new toys.

They rushed forward and seized Cadj. They talked in loud menacing tones into his ear. They threatened him with bludgeon and knife until at last he acquiesced in their demands, though sullenly, and then Tarzan stepped close before Cadj.

"Priest," he said, "La goes back to her temple under the protection of her priests and the threat of Tarzan of the Apes that whoever harms her shall die. Tarzan will go again to Opar before the next rains and if harm has befallen La, woe betide Cadj, the High Priest."

Sullenly Cadj promised not to harm his queen.

"Protect her," cried Tarzan to the other Oparians. "Protect her so that when Tarzan comes again he will find La there to greet him."

"La will be there to greet thee," exclaimed the High Priestess, "and La will wait, longing, always longing, until you come again. Oh, tell me that you will come!"

"Who knows?" asked the ape-man as he swung quickly into the trees and raced off toward the east.

For a moment La stood looking after him, then her head drooped, a sigh escaped her lips and like an old woman she took up the march toward distant Opar.

Through the trees raced Tarzan of the Apes until the darkness of night had settled upon the jungle, then he lay down and slept, with no thought beyond the morrow and with even La but the shadow of a memory within his consciousness.

But a few marches to the north Lady Greystoke looked forward to the day when her mighty lord and master should discover the crime of Achmet Zek, and be speeding to rescue and avenge, and even as she pictured the coming of John Clayton, the object of her thoughts squatted almost naked, beside a fallen log, beneath which he was searching with grimy fingers for a chance beetle or a luscious grub.

Two days elapsed following the theft of the jewels before Tarzan gave them a thought. Then, as they chanced to enter his mind, he conceived a desire to play with them again, and, having nothing better to do than satisfy the first whim which possessed him, he rose and started across the plain from the forest in which he had spent the preceding day.

Though no mark showed where the gems had been buried, and though the spot resembled the balance of an unbroken stretch several miles in length, where the reeds terminated at the edge of the meadowland, yet the ape-man moved with unerring precision directly to the place where he had hid his treasure.

With his hunting knife he upturned the loose earth, beneath which the pouch should be; but, though he excavated to a greater distance than the depth of the original hole there was no sign of pouch or jewels. Tarzan's brow clouded as he discovered that he had been despoiled. Little or no reasoning was required to convince him of the identity of the guilty party, and with the same celerity that had marked his decision to unearth the jewels, he set out upon the trail of the thief.

Though the spoor was two days old, and practically obliterated in many places, Tarzan followed it with comparative ease. A white man could not have followed it twenty paces twelve hours after it had been made, a black man would have lost it within the first mile; but Tarzan of the Apes had been forced in childhood to develop senses that an ordinary mortal scarce ever uses.

We may note the garlic and whisky on the breath of a fellow strap hanger, or the cheap perfume emanating from the person of the wondrous lady sitting in front of us, and deplore the fact of our sensitive noses; but, as a matter of fact, we cannot smell at all, our olfactory organs are practically atrophied, by comparison with the development of the sense among the beasts of the wild.

Where a foot is placed an effluvium remains for a considerable time. It is beyond the range of our sensibilities; but to a creature of the lower orders, especially to the hunters and the hunted, as interesting and ofttimes more lucid than is the printed page to us.

Nor was Tarzan dependant alone upon his sense of smell. Vision and hearing had been brought to a marvelous state of development by the necessities of his early life, where survival itself depended almost daily upon the exercise of the keenest vigilance and the constant use of all his faculties.

And so he followed the old trail of the Belgian through the forest and toward the north; but because of the age of the trail he was constrained to a far from rapid progress. The man he followed was two days ahead of him when Tarzan took up the pursuit, and each day he gained upon the ape-man. The latter, however, felt not the slightest doubt as to the outcome. Some day he would overhaul his quarry —he could bide his time in peace until that day dawned. Doggedly he followed the faint spoor, pausing by day only to kill and eat, and at night only to sleep and refresh himself.

Occasionally he passed parties of savage warriors; but these he gave a wide berth, for he was hunting with a purpose that was not to be distracted by the minor accidents of the trail.

These parties were of the collecting hordes of the Waziri and their allies which Basuli had scattered his messengers broadcast to summon. They were marching to a common rendezvous in preparation for an assault upon the stronghold of Achmet Zek; but to Tarzan they were enemies—he retained no conscious memory of any friendship for the black men.

It was night when he halted outside the palisaded village of the Arab raider. Perched in the branches of a great tree he gazed down upon the life within the enclosure. To this place had the spoor led him. His quarry must be within; but how was he to find him among so many huts? Tarzan, although cognizant of his mighty powers, realized also his limitations. He knew that he could not successfully cope with great numbers in open battle. He must resort to the stealth and trickery of the wild beast, if he were to succeed.

Sitting in the safety of his tree, munching upon the leg bone of Horta, the boar, Tarzan, waited a favorable opportunity to enter the village. For awhile he gnawed at the bulging, round ends of the large bone, splintering off small pieces between his strong jaws, and sucking at the delicious marrow within; but all the time he cast repeated glances into the village. He saw white-robed figures, and half-naked blacks; but not once did he see one who resembled the stealer of the gems.

Patiently he waited until the streets were deserted by all save the sentries at the gates, then he dropped lightly to the ground, circled to the opposite side of the village an approached the palisade.

At his side hung a long, rawhide rope—a natural and more dependable evolution from the grass rope of his childhood. Loosening this, he spread the noose upon the ground behind him, and with a quick movement of his wrist tossed the coils over one of the sharpened projections of the summit of the palisade.

Drawing the noose taut, he tested the solidity of its hold. Satisfied, the ape-man ran nimbly up the vertical wall, aided by the rope which he clutched in both hands. Once at the top it required but a moment to gather the dangling rope once more into its coils, make it fast again at his waist, take a quick glance downward within the palisade, and, assured that no one lurked directly beneath him, drop softly to the ground.

Now he was within the village. Before him stretched a series of tents and native huts. The business of exploring each of them would be fraught with danger; but danger was only a natural factor of each day's life—it never appalled Tarzan. The chances appealed to him—the chances of life and death, with his prowess and his faculties pitted against those of a worthy antagonist.

It was not necessary that he enter each habitation—through a door, a window or an open chink, his nose told him whether or no his prey lay within. For some time he found one disappointment following upon the heels of another in quick succession. No spoor of the Belgian was discernible. But at last he came to a tent where the smell of the thief was strong. Tarzan listened, his ear close to the canvas at the rear, but no sound came from within.

At last he cut one of the pin ropes, raised the bottom of the canvas, and intruded his head within the interior. All was quiet and dark. Tarzan crawled cautiously within—the scent of the Belgian was strong; but it was not live scent. Even before he had examined the interior minutely, Tarzan knew that no one was within it.

In one corner he found a pile of blankets and clothing scattered about; but no pouch of pretty pebbles. A careful examination of the balance of the tent revealed nothing more, at least nothing to indicate the presence of the jewels; but at the side where the blankets and clothing lay, the ape-man discovered that the tent wall had been loosened at the bottom, and presently he sensed that the Belgian had recently passed out of the tent by this avenue.

Tarzan was not long in following the way that his prey had fled. The spoor led always in the shadow and at the rear of the huts and tents of the village—it was quite evident to Tarzan that the Belgian had gone alone and secretly upon his mission. Evidently he feared the inhabitants of the village, or at least his work had been of such a nature that he dared not risk detection.

At the back of a native hut the spoor led through a

small hole recently cut in the brush wall and into the dark interior beyond. Fearlessly, Tarzan followed the trail. On hands and knees he crawled through the small aperture. Within the hut his nostrils were assailed by many odors; but clear and distinct among them was one that half aroused a latent memory of the past—it was the faint and delicate odor of a woman. With the cognizance of it there rose in the breast of the ape-man a strange uneasiness—the result of an irresistible force which he was destined to become acquainted with anew—the instinct which draws the male to his mate.

In the same hut was the scent spoor of the Belgian, too, and as both these assailed the nostrils of the ape-man, mingling one with the other, a jealous rage leaped and burned within him, though his memory held before the mirror of recollection no image of the she to which he had attached his desire.

Like the tent he had investigated, the hut, too, was empty, and after satisfying himself that his stolen pouch was secreted nowhere within, he left, as he had entered, by the hole in the rear wall.

Here he took up the spoor of the Belgian, followed it across the clearing, over the palisade, and out into the dark jungle beyond.

15

The Flight of Werper

AFTER Werper had arranged the dummy in his bed, and sneaked out into the darkness of the village beneath the rear wall of his tent, he had gone directly to the hut in which Jane Clayton was held captive.

Before the doorway squatted a black sentry. Werper approached him boldly, spoke a few words in his ear, handed him a package of tobacco, and passed into the hut. The black grinned and winked as the European disappeared within the darkness of the interior.

The Belgian, being one of Achmet Zek's principal lieutenants, might naturally go where he wished within or without the village, and so the sentry had not questioned his right to enter the hut with the white, woman prisoner.

Within, Werper called in French and in a low whisper: "Lady

Greystoke! It is I, M. Frecoult. Where are you?" But there was
no response. Hastily the man felt around the interior, groping
blindly through the darkness with outstretched hands. There
was no one within!

Werper's astonishment surpassed words. He was on the point
of stepping without to question the sentry, when his eyes, becoming accustomed to the dark, discovered a blotch of lesser
blackness near the base of the rear wall of the hut. Examination
revealed the fact that the blotch was an opening cut in the
wall. It was large enough to permit the passage of his body, and,
assured as he was, that Lady Greystoke had passed out through
the aperture in an attempt to escape the village, he lost no
time in availing himself of the same avenue; but neither did
he lose time in a fruitless search for Jane Clayton.

His own life depended upon the chance of his eluding, or
outdistancing Achmet Zek, when that worthy should have discovered that he had escaped. His original plan had contemplated connivance in the escape of Lady Greystoke for two
very good and sufficient reasons. The first was that by saving
her he would win the gratitude of the English, and thus lessen
the chance of his extradition should his identity and his
crime against his superior officer be charged against him.

The second reason was based upon the fact that only one
direction of escape was safely open to him. He could not travel
to the west because of the Belgian possessions which lay between him and the Atlantic. The south was closed to him by the
feared presence of the savage ape-man he had robbed. To
the north lay the friends and allies of Achmet Zek. Only toward
the east, through British East Africa, lay reasonable assurance
of freedom.

Accompanied by a titled Englishwoman whom he had rescued from a frightful fate, and his identity vouched for by her
as that of a Frenchman by the name of Frecoult, he had
looked forward, and not without reason, to the active assistance of the British from the moment that he came in
contact with their first outpost.

But now that Lady Greystoke had disappeared, though he still
looked toward the east for hope, his chances were lessened,
and another, subsidiary design completely dashed. From the
moment that he had first laid eyes upon Jane Clayton he had
nursed within his breast a secret passion for the beautiful
American wife of the English lord, and when Achmet Zek's
discovery of the jewels had necessitated flight, the Belgian had
dreamed, in his planning, of a future in which he might convince Lady Greystoke that her husband was dead, and by
playing upon her gratitude win her for himself.

At that part of the village farthest from the gates, Werper

discovered that two or three long poles, taken from a nearby pile which had been collected for the construction of huts, had been leaned against the top of the palisade, forming a precarious, though not impossible avenue of escape.

Rightly, he inferred that thus had Lady Greystoke found the means to scale the wall, nor did he lose even a moment in following her lead. Once in the jungle he struck out directly eastward.

A few miles south of him, Jane Clayton lay panting among the branches of a tree in which she had taken refuge from a prowling and hungry lioness.

Her escape from the village had been much easier than she had anticipated. The knife which she had used to cut her way through the brush wall of the hut to freedom, she had found sticking in the wall of her prison, doubtless left there by accident when a former tenant had vacated the premises.

To cross the rear of the village, keeping always in the densest shadows, had required but a few moments, and the fortunate circumstance of the discovery of the hut poles lying so near the palisade had solved for her the problem of the passage of the high wall.

For an hour she had followed the old game trail toward the south, until there fell upon her trained hearing the stealthy padding of a stalking beast behind her. The nearest tree gave her instant sanctuary, for she was too wise in the ways of the jungle to chance her safety for a moment after discovering that she was being hunted.

Werper, with better success, traveled slowly onward until dawn, when, to his chagrin, he discovered a mounted Arab upon his trail. It was one of Achmet Zek's minions, many of whom were scattered in all directions through the forest, searching for the fugitive Belgian.

Jane Clayton's escape had not yet been discovered when Achmet Zek and his searchers set forth to overhaul Werper. The only man who had seen the Belgian after his departure from his tent was the black sentry before the doorway of Lady Greystoke's prison hut, and he had been silenced by the discovery of the dead body of the man who had relieved him, the sentry that Mugambi had dispatched.

The bribe taker naturally inferred that Werper had slain his fellow and dared not admit that he had permitted him to enter the hut, fearing as he did, the anger of Achmet Zek. So, as chance directed that he should be the one to discover the body of the sentry when the first alarm had been given following Achmet Zek's discovery that Werper had outwitted him, the crafty black had dragged the dead body to the interior of a nearby tent, and himself resumed his station before the doorway of the hut in which he still believed the woman to be.

With the discovery of the Arab close behind him, the Belgian hid in the foliage of a leafy bush. Here the trail ran straight for a considerable distance, and down the shady forest aisle, beneath the overarching branches of the trees, rode the white-robed figure of the pursuer.

Nearer and nearer he came. Werper crouched closer to the ground behind the leaves of his hiding place. Across the trail a vine moved. Werper's eyes instantly centered upon the spot. There was no wind to stir the foliage in the depths of the jungle. Again the vine moved. In the mind of the Belgian only the presence of a sinister and malevolent force could account for the phenomenon.

The man's eyes bored steadily into the screen of leaves upon the opposite side of the trail. Gradually a form took shape beyond them—a tawny form, grim and terrible, with yellow-green eyes glaring fearsomely across the narrow trail straight into his.

Werper could have screamed in fright, but up the trail was coming the messenger of another death, equally sure and no less terrible. He remained silent, almost paralyzed by fear. The Arab approached. Across the trail from Werper the lion crouched for the spring, when suddenly his attention was attracted toward the horseman.

The Belgian saw the massive head turn in the direction of the raider and his heart all but ceased its beating as he waited the result of this interruption. At a walk the horseman approached. Would the nervous animal he rode take fright at the odor of the carnivore, and, bolting, leave Werper still to the mercies of the king of beasts?

But he seemed unmindful of the near presence of the great cat. On he came, his neck arched, champing at the bit between his teeth. The Belgian turned his eyes again toward the lion. The beast's whole attention now seemed riveted upon the horseman. They were abreast the lion now, and still the brute did not spring. Could he be but waiting for them to pass before returning his attention to the original prey? Werper shuddered and half rose. At the same instant the lion sprang from his place of concealment, full upon the mounted man. The horse, with a shrill neigh of terror, shrank sideways almost upon the Belgian, the lion dragged the helpless Arab from his saddle, and the horse leaped back into the trail and fled away toward the west.

But he did not flee alone. As the frightened beast had pressed in upon him, Werper had not been slow to note the quickly emptied saddle and the opportunity it presented. Scarcely had the lion dragged the Arab down from one side, than the Belgian, seizing the pommel of the saddle and the horse's mane, leaped upon the horse's back from the other.

A half hour later a naked giant, swinging easily through the lower branches of the trees, paused, and with raised head, and dilating nostrils sniffed the morning air. The smell of blood fell strong upon his sense, and mingled with it was the scent of Numa, the lion. The giant cocked his head upon one side and listened.

From a short distance up the trail came the unmistakable noises of the greedy feeding of a lion. The crunching of bones, the gulping of great pieces, the contented growling, all attested the nearness of the king at table.

Tarzan approached the spot, still keeping to the branches of the trees. He made no effort to conceal his approach, and presently he had evidence that Numa had heard him, from the ominous, rumbling warning that broke from a thicket beside the trail.

Halting upon a low branch just above the lion Tarzan looked down upon the grisly scene. Could this unrecognizable thing be the man he had been trailing? The ape-man wondered. From time to time he had descended to the trail and verified his judgment by the evidence of his scent that the Belgian had followed this game trail toward the east.

Now he proceeded beyond the lion and his feast, again descended and examined the ground with his nose. There was no scent spoor here of the man he had been trailing. Tarzan returned to the tree. With keen eyes he searched the ground about the mutilated corpse for a sign of the missing pouch of pretty pebbles; but naught could he see of it.

He scolded Numa and tried to drive the great beast away; but only angry growls rewarded his efforts. He tore small branches from a nearby limb and hurled them at his ancient enemy. Numa looked up with bared fangs, grinning hideously, but he did not rise from his kill.

Then Tarzan fitted an arrow to his bow, and drawing the slim shaft far back let drive with all the force of the tough wood that only he could bend. As the arrow sank deeply into his side, Numa leaped to his feet with a roar of mingled rage and pain. He leaped futilely at the grinning ape-man, tore at the protruding end of the shaft, and then, springing into the trail, paced back and forth beneath his tormentor. Again Tarzan loosed a swift bolt. This time the missile, aimed with care, lodged in the lion's spine. The great creature halted in its tracks, and lurched awkwardly forward upon its face, paralyzed.

Tarzan dropped to the trail, ran quickly to the beast's side, and drove his spear deep into the fierce heart, then after re-covering his arrows turned his attention to the mutilated re-mains of the animal's prey in the nearby thicket.

The face was gone. The Arab garments aroused no doubt as to the man's identity, since he had trailed him into the Arab camp and out again, where he might easily have ac-quired the apparel. So sure was Tarzan that the body was that of he who had robbed him that he made no effort to verify his deductions by scent among the conglomerate odors of the great carnivore and the fresh blood of the victim.

He confined his attentions to a careful search for the pouch, but nowhere upon or about the corpse was any sign of the missing article or its contents. The ape-man was dis-appointed—possibly not so much because of the loss of the colored pebbles as with Numa for robbing him of the pleas-ures of revenge.

Wondering what could have become of his possessions, the ape-man turned slowly back along the trail in the di-rection from which he had come. In his mind he revolved a plan to enter and search the Arab camp, after darkness had again fallen. Taking to the trees, he moved directly south in search of prey, that he might satisfy his hunger before mid-day, and then lie up for the afternoon in some spot far from the camp, where he might sleep without fear of discovery until it came time to prosecute his design.

Scarcely had he quitted the trail when a tall, black warrior, moving at a dogged trot, passed toward the east. It was Mugambi, searching for his mistress. He continued along the trail, halting to examine the body of the dead lion. An ex-pression of puzzlement crossed his features as he bent to search for the wounds which had caused the death of the jungle lord. Tarzan had removed his arrows, but to Mugambi the proof of death was as strong as though both the lighter missiles and the spear still protruded from the carcass.

The black looked furtively about him. The body was still warm, and from this fact he reasoned that the killer was close at hand, yet no sign of living man appeared. Mugambi shook his head, and continued along the trail, but with re-doubled caution.

All day he traveled, stopping occasionally to call aloud the single word, "Lady," in the hope that at last she might hear and respond; but in the end his loyal devotion brought him to disaster.

From the northeast, for several months, Abdul Mourak, in command of a detachment of Abyssinian soldiers, had been assiduously searching for the Arab raider, Achmet Zek, who, six months previously, had affronted the majesty of Abdul

Mourak's emperor by conducting a slave raid within the boundaries of Menelek's domain.

And now it happened that Abdul Mourak had halted for a short rest at noon upon this very day and along the same trail that Werper and Mugambi were following toward the east.

It was shortly after the soldiers had dismounted that the Belgian, unaware of their presence, rode his tired mount almost into their midst, before he had discovered them. Instantly he was surrounded, and a volley of questions hurled at him, as he was pulled from his horse and led toward the presence of the commander.

Falling back upon his European nationality, Werper assured Abdul Mourak that he was a Frenchman, hunting in Africa, and that he had been attacked by strangers, his safari killed or scattered, and himself escaping only by a miracle.

From a chance remark of the Abyssinian, Werper discovered the purpose of the expedition, and when he realized that these men were the enemies of Achmet Zek, he took heart, and immediately blamed his predicament upon the Arab.

Lest, however, he might again fall into the hands of the raider, he discouraged Abdul Mourak in the further prosecution of his pursuit, assuring the Abyssinian that Achmet Zek commanded a large and dangerous force, and also that he was marching rapidly toward the south.

Convinced that it would take a long time to overhaul the raider, and that the chances of engagement made the outcome extremely questionable, Mourak, none too unwillingly, abandoned his plan and gave the necessary orders for his command to pitch camp where they were, preparatory to taking up the return march toward Abyssinia the following morning.

It was late in the afternoon that the attention of the camp was attracted toward the west by the sound of a powerful voice calling a single word, repeated several times: "Lady! Lady! Lady!"

True to their instincts of precaution, a number of Abyssinians, acting under orders from Abdul Mourak, advanced stealthily through the jungle toward the author of the call.

A half hour later they returned, dragging Mugambi among them. The first person the big black's eyes fell upon as he was hustled into the presence of the Abyssinian officer, was M. Jules Frecoult, the Frenchman who had been the guest of his master and whom he last had seen entering the village of Achmet Zek under circumstances which pointed his familiarity and friendship for the raiders.

Between the disasters that had befallen his master and his

master's house, and the Frenchman, Mugambi saw a sinister relationship, which kept him from recalling to Werper's attention the identity which the latter evidently failed to recognize.

Pleading that he was but a harmless hunter from a tribe farther south, Mugambi begged to be allowed to go upon his way; but Abdul Mourak, admiring the warrior's splendid physique, decided to take him back to Adis Abeba and present him to Menelek. A few moments later Mugambi and Werper were marched away under guard, and the Belgian learned for the first time, that he too was a prisoner rather than a guest. In vain he protested against such treatment, until a strapping soldier struck him across the mouth and threatened to shoot him if he did not desist.

Mugambi took the matter less to heart, for he had not the slightest doubt but that during the course of the journey he would find ample opportunity to elude the vigilance of his guards and make good his escape. With this idea always uppermost in his mind, he courted the good opinion of the Abyssinians, asked them many questions about their emperor and their country, and evinced a growing desire to reach their destination, that he might enjoy all the good things which they assured him the city of Adis Abeba contained. Thus he disarmed their suspicions, and each day found a slight relaxation of their watchfulness over him.

By taking advantage of the fact that he and Werper always were kept together, Mugambi sought to learn what the other knew of the whereabouts of Tarzan, or the authorship of the raid upon the bungalow, as well as the fate of Lady Greystoke; but as he was confined to the accidents of conversation for this information, not daring to acquaint Werper with his true identity, and as Werper was equally anxious to conceal from the world his part in the destruction of his host's home and happiness, Mugambi learned nothing—at least in this way.

But there came a time when he learned a very surprising thing, by accident.

The party had camped early in the afternoon of a sultry day, upon the banks of a clear and beautiful stream. The bottom of the river was gravelly, there was no indication of crocodiles, those menaces to promiscuous bathing in the rivers of certain portions of the dark continent, and so the Abyssinians took advantage of the opportunity to perform long-deferred, and much needed, ablutions.

As Werper, who, with Mugambi, had been given permission to enter the water, removed his clothing, the black noted the care with which he unfastened something which circled his waist, and which he took off with his shirt, keeping the latter always around and concealing the object of his suspicious solicitude.

It was this very carefulness which attracted the black's attention to the thing, arousing a natural curiosity in the warrior's mind, and so it chanced that when the Belgian, in the nervousness of overcaution, fumbled the hidden article and dropped it. Mugambi saw it as it fell upon the ground, spilling a portion of its contents on the sward.

Now Mugambi had been to London with his master. He was not the unsophisticated savage that his apparel proclaimed him. He had mingled with the cosmopolitan hordes of the greatest city in the world; he had visited museums and inspected shop windows; and, besides, he was a shrewd and intelligent man.

The instant that the jewels of Opar rolled, scintillating, before his astonished eyes, he recognized them for what they were; but he recognized something else, too, that interested him far more deeply than the value of the stones. A thousand times he had seen the leathern pouch which dangled at his master's side, when Tarzan of the Apes had, in a spirit of play and adventure, elected to return for a few hours to the primitive manners and customs of his boyhood, and surrounded by his naked warriors hunt the lion and the leopard, the buffalo and the elephant after the manner he loved best.

Werper saw that Mugambi had seen the pouch and the stones. Hastily he gathered up the precious gems and returned them to their container, while Mugambi, assuming an air of indifference, strolled down to the river for his bath.

The following morning Abdul Mourak was enraged and chagrined to discover that his huge, black prisoner had escaped during the night, while Werper was terrified for the same reason, until his trembling fingers discovered the pouch still in its place beneath his shirt, and within it the hard outlines of its contents.

16

Tarzan Again Leads the Mangani

ACHMET ZEK with two of his followers had circled far to the south to intercept the flight of his deserting lieutenant, Werper. Others had spread out in various directions, so that a vast circle had been formed by them during the night, and now they were beating in toward the center.

Achmet and the two with him halted for a short rest just before noon. They squatted beneath the trees upon the southern edge of a clearing. The chief of the raiders was in ill humor. To have been outwitted by an unbeliever was bad enough; but to have, at the same time, lost the jewels upon which he had set his avaricious heart was altogether too much—Allah must, indeed, be angry with his servant.

Well, he still had the woman. She would bring a fair price in the north, and there was, too, the buried treasure beside the ruins of the Englishman's house.

A slight noise in the jungle upon the opposite side of the clearing brought Achmet Zek to immediate and alert attention. He gathered his rifle in readiness for instant use, at the same time motioning his followers to silence and concealment. Crouching behind bushes the three waited, their eyes fastened upon the far side of the open space.

Presently the foliage parted and a woman's face appeared, glancing fearfully from side to side. A moment later, evidently satisfied that no immediate danger lurked before her, she stepped out into the clearing in full view of the Arab.

Achmet Zek caught his breath with a muttered exclamation of incredulity and an imprecation. The woman was the prisoner he had thought safely guarded at his camp!

Apparently she was alone, but Achmet Zek waited that he might make sure of it before seizing her. Slowly Jane Clayton started across the clearing. Twice already since she had quitted the village of the raiders had she barely escaped the fangs of carnivora, and once she had almost stumbled into the path of one of the searchers. Though she was almost despairing of ever reaching safety she still was determined to fight on, until death or success terminated her endeavors.

As the Arabs watched her from the safety of their concealment, and Achmet Zek noted with satisfaction that she was walking directly into his clutches, another pair of eyes looked down upon the entire scene from the foliage of an adjacent tree.

Puzzled, troubled eyes they were, for all their gray and savage glint, for their owner was struggling with an intangible suggestion of the familiarity of the face and figure of the woman below him.

A sudden crashing of the bushes at the point from which Jane Clayton had emerged into the clearing brough her to a sudden stop and attracted the attention of the Arabs and the watcher in the tree to the same point.

The woman wheeled about to see what new danger menaced her from behind, and as she did so a great, anthropoid ape waddled into view. Behind him came another and another; but Lady Greystoke did not wait to learn how many more of the hideous creatures were so close upon her trail.

With a smothered scream she rushed toward the opposite jungle, and as she reached the bushes there, Achmet Zek and his two henchmen rose up and seized her. At the same instant a naked, brown giant dropped from the branches of a tree at the right of the clearing.

Turning toward the astonished apes he gave voice to a short volley of low gutturals, and without waiting to note the effect of his words upon them, wheeled and charged for the Arabs.

Achmet Zek was dragging Jane Clayton toward his tethered horse. His two men were hastily unfastening all three mounts. The woman, struggling to escape the Arab, turned and saw the ape-man running toward her. A glad light of hope illumined her face.

"John!" she cried. "Thank God that you have come in time."

Behind Tarzan came the great apes, wondering, but obedient to his summons. The Arabs saw that they would not have time to mount and make their escape before the beasts and the man were upon them. Achmet Zek recognized the latter as the redoubtable enemy of such as he, and he saw too in the circumstance an opportunity to rid himself forever of the menace of the ape-man's presence.

Calling to his men to follow his example he raised his rifle and leveled it upon the charging giant. His followers, acting with no less alacrity than himself, fired almost simultaneously, and with the reports of the rifles, Tarzan of the Apes and two of his hairy henchmen pitched forward among the jungle grasses.

The noise of the rifle shots brought the balance of the apes to a wondering pause, and, taking advantage of their momentary distraction, Achmet Zek and his fellows leaped to their horses' backs and galloped away with the now hopeless and grief-stricken woman.

Back to the village they rode, and once again Lady Greystoke found herself incarcerated in the filthy, little hut from which she had thought to have escaped for good. But this time she was not only guarded by an additional sentry, but bound as well.

Singly and in twos the searchers who had ridden out with Achmet Zek upon the trail of the Belgian, returned empty handed. With the report of each the raider's rage and chagrin increased, until he was in such a transport of ferocious anger that none dared approach him. Threatening and cursing, Achmet Zek paced up and down the floor of his silken tent; but his temper served him naught—Werper was gone and with him the fortune in scintillating gems which had aroused the cupidity of his chief and placed the sentence of death upon the head of the lieutenant.

With the escape of the Arabs the great apes had turned their attention to their fallen comrades. One was dead, but another and the great white ape still breathed. The hairy monsters gathered about these two, grumbling and muttering after the fashion of their kind.

Tarzan was the first to regain consciousness. Sitting up, he looked about him. Blood was flowing from a wound in his shoulder. The shock had thrown him down and dazed him; but he was far from dead. Rising slowly to his feet he let his eyes wander toward the spot where last he had seen the she, who had aroused within his savage breast such strange emotions.

"Where is she?" he asked.

"The Tarmangani took her away," replied one of the apes. "Who are you who speak the language of the Mangani?"

"I am Tarzan," replied the ape-man; "mighty hunter, greatest of fighters. When I roar, the jungle is silent and trembles with terror. I am Tarzan of the Apes. I have been away; but now I have come back to my people."

"Yes," spoke up an old ape, "he is Tarzan. I know him. It is well that he has come back. Now we shall have good hunting."

The other apes came closer and sniffed at the ape-man. Tarzan stood very still, his fangs half bared, and his muscles tense and ready for action; but there was none there to question his right to be with them, and presently, the inspection satisfactorily concluded, the apes again returned their attention to the other survivor.

He too was but slightly wounded, a bullet, grazing his skull, having stunned him, so that when he regained consciousness he was apparently as fit as ever.

The apes told Tarzan that they had been traveling toward the east when the scent spoor of the she had attracted them and they had stalked her. Now they wished to continue upon their interrupted march; but Tarzan preferred to follow the Arabs and take the woman from them. After a considerable argument it was decided that they should first hunt toward the east for a few days and then return and search for the Arabs, and as time is of little moment to the ape folk, Tarzan acceded to their demands, he, himself, having reverted to a mental state but little superior to their own.

Another circumstance which decided him to postpone pursuit of the Arabs was the painfulness of his wound. It would be better to wait until that had healed before he pitted himself again against the guns of the Tarmangani.

And so, as Jane Clayton was pushed into her prison hut and her hands and feet securely bound, her natural protector roamed off toward the east in company with a score of hairy monsters, with whom he rubbed shoulders as familiarly as a few months before he had mingled with his immaculate fellow-members of one of London's most select and exclusive clubs.

But all the time there lurked in the back of his injured brain a troublesome conviction that he had no business where he was—that he should be, for some unaccountable reason, elsewhere and among another sort of creature. Also, there was the compelling urge to be upon the scent of the Arabs, undertaking the rescue of the woman who had appealed so strongly to his savage sentiments; though the thought-word which naturally occurred to him in the contemplation of the venture, was "capture," rather than "rescue."

To him she was as any other jungle she, and he had set his heart upon her as his mate. For an instant, as he had approached closer to her in the clearing where the Arabs had seized her, the subtle aroma which had first aroused his desires in the hut that had imprisoned her had fallen upon his nostrils, and told him that he had found the creature for whom he had developed so sudden and inexplicable a passion.

The matter of the pouch of jewels also occupied his thoughts to some extent, so that he found a double urge for his return to the camp of the raiders. He would obtain possession of both his pretty pebbles and the she. Then he would return to the great apes with his new mate and his baubles, and leading his hairy companions into a far wilderness beyond the ken of man, live out his life, hunting and battling among the lower orders after the only manner which he now recollected.

He spoke to his fellow-apes upon the matter, in an attempt to persuade them to accompany him; but all except Taglat and Chulk refused. The latter was young and strong, endowed with a greater intelligence than his fellows, and therefore the possessor of better developed powers of imagination. To him the expedition savored of adventure, and so appealed, strongly. With Taglat there was another incentive—a secret and sinister incentive, which, had Tarzan of the Apes had knowledge of it, would have sent him at the other's throat in jealous rage.

Taglat was no longer young; but he was still a formidable

beast, mightily muscled, cruel, and, because of his greater
experience, crafty and cunning. Too, he was of giant proportions, the very weight of his huge bulk serving ofttimes to
discount in his favor the superior agility of a younger antagonist.

He was of a morose and sullen disposition that marked
him even among his frowning fellows, where such characteristics are the rule rather than the exception, and, though
Tarzan did not guess it, he hated the ape-man with a ferocity
that he was able to hide only because the dominant spirit of
the nobler creature had inspired within him a species of
dread which was as powerful as it was inexplicable to him.

These two, then, were to be Tarzan's companions upon his
return to the village of Achmet Zek. As they set off, the
balance of the tribe vouchsafed them but a parting stare, and
then resumed the serious business of feeding.

Tarzan found difficulty in keeping the minds of his fellows set upon the purpose of their adventure, for the mind
of an ape lacks the power of long-sustained concentration.
To set out upon a long journey, with a definite destination
in view, is one thing, to remember that purpose and keep it
uppermost in one's mind continually is quite another. There
are so many things to distract one's attention along the way.

Chulk was, at first, for rushing rapidly ahead as though
the village of the raiders lay but an hour's march before
them instead of several days; but within a few minutes a
fallen tree attracted his attention with its suggestion of rich
and succulent forage beneath, and when Tarzan, missing him,
returned in search, he found Chulk squatting beside the
rotting bole, from beneath which he was assiduously engaged in digging out the grubs and beetles, whose kind form
a considerable proportion of the diet of the apes.

Unless Tarzan desired to fight there was nothing to do but
wait until Chulk had exhausted the storehouse, and this he
did, only to discover that Taglet was now missing. After a
considerable search, he found that worthy gentleman con-
templating the sufferings of an injured rodent he had
pounced upon. He would sit in apparent indifference, gazing
in another direction, while the crippled creature wriggled
slowly and painfully away from him, and then, just as his
victim felt assured of escape, he would reach out a giant
palm and slam it down upon the fugitive. Again and again
he repeated this operation, until, tiring of the sport, he
ended the sufferings of his plaything by devouring it.

Such were the exasperating causes of delay which retarded
Tarzan's return journey toward the village of Achmet Zek; but
the ape-man was patient, for in his mind was a plan which

necessitated the presence of Chulk and Taglat when he should have arrived at his destination.

It was not always an easy thing to maintain in the vacillating minds of the anthropoids a sustained interest in their venture. Chulk was wearying of the continued marching and the infrequency and short duration of the rests. He would gladly have abandoned this search for adventure had not Tarzan continually filled his mind with alluring pictures of the great stores of food which were to be found in the village of the Tarmangani.

Taglat nursed his secret purpose to better advantage than might have been expected of an ape, yet there were times when he, too, would have abandoned the adventure had not Tarzan cajoled him on.

It was mid-afternoon of a sultry, tropical day when the keen senses of the three warned them of the proximity of the Arab camp. Stealthily they approached, keeping to the dense tangle of growing things which made concealment easy to their uncanny jungle craft.

First came the giant ape-man, his smooth, brown skin glistening with the sweat of exertion in the close, hot confines of the jungle. Behind him crept Chulk and Taglat, grotesque and shaggy caricatures of their godlike leader.

Silently they made their way to the edge of the clearing which surrounded the palisade, and here they clambered into the lower branches of a large tree overlooking the village occupied by the enemy, the better to spy upon his goings and comings.

A horseman, white burnoosed, rode out through the gateway of the village. Tarzan, whispering to Chulk and Taglat to remain where they were, swung, monkey-like, through the trees in the direction of the trail the Arab was riding. From one jungle giant to the next he sped with the rapidity of a squirrel and the silence of a ghost.

The Arab rode slowly onward, unconscious of the danger hovering in the trees behind him. The ape-man made a slight détour and increased his speed until he had reached a point upon the trail in advance of the horseman. Here he halted upon a leafy bough which overhung the narrow, jungle trail. On came the victim, humming a wild air of the great desert land of the north. Above him poised the savage brute that was today bent upon the destruction of a human life—the same creature who a few months before, had occupied his seat in the House of Lords at London, a respected and distinguished member of that august body.

The Arab passed beneath the overhanging bough, there was a slight rustling of the leaves above, the horse snorted and plunged as a brown-skinned creature dropped upon its rump. A pair of mighty arms encircled the Arab and he was dragged from his saddle to the trail.

Ten minutes later the ape-man, carrying the outer garments of an Arab bundled beneath an arm, rejoined his companions. He exhibited his trophies to them, explaining in low gutterals the details of his exploit. Chulk and Taglat fingered the fabrics, smelled of them, and, placing them to their ears, tried to listen to them.

Then Tarzan led them back through the jungle to the trail, where the three hid themselves and waited. Nor had they long to wait before two of Achmet Zek's blacks, clothed in habiliments similar to their master's, came down the trail on foot, returning to the camp.

One moment they were laughing and talking together— the next they lay stretched in death upon the trail, three mighty engines of destruction bending over them. Tarzan removed their outer garments as he had removed those of his first victim, and again retired with Chulk and Taglat to the greater seclusion of the tree they had first selected.

Here the ape-man arranged the garments upon his shaggy fellows and himself, until, at a distance, it might have appeared that three white-robed Arabs squatted silently among the branches of the forest.

Until dark they remained where they were, for from his point of vantage, Tarzan could view the enclosure within the palisade. He marked the position of the hut in which he had first discovered the scent-spoor of the she he sought. He saw the two sentries standing before its doorway, and he located the habitation of Achmet Zek, where something told him he would most likely find his missing pouch and pebbles.

Chulk and Taglat were, at first, greatly interested in their wonderful raiment. They fingered the fabric, smelled of it, and regarded each other intently with every mark of satisfaction and pride. Chulk, a humorist in his way, stretched forth a long and hairy arm, and grasping the hood of Taglat's burnoose pulled it down over the latter's eyes, extinguishing him, snuffer-like, as it were.

The older ape, pessimistic by nature, recognized no such thing as humor. Creatures laid their paws upon him for but two things—to search for fleas and to attack. The pulling of the Tarmangani-scented thing about his head and eyes could not be for the performance of the former act; therefore it must be the latter. He was attacked! Chulk had attacked him.

With a snarl he was at the other's throat, not even waiting to lift the woolen veil which obscured his vision. Tarzan leaped upon the two, and swaying and toppling upon their insecure perch the three great beasts tussled and snapped at one another until the ape-man finally succeeded in separating the enraged anthropoids.

An apology is unknown to these savage progenitors of man, and explanation a laborious and usually futile process, Tarzan bridged the dangerous gulf by distracting their attention from their altercation to a consideration of their plans for the immediate future. Accustomed to frequent arguments in which more hair than blood is wasted, the apes speedily forget such trivial encounters, and presently Chulk and Taglat were again squatting in close proximity to each other and peaceful repose, awaiting the moment when the ape-man should lead them into the village of the Tarmangani.

It was long after darkness had fallen, that Tarzan led his companions from their hiding place in the tree to the ground and around the palisade to the far side of the village.

Gathering the skirts of his burnoose, beneath one arm, that his legs might have free action, the ape-man took a short running start, and scrambled to the top of the barrier. Fearing lest the apes should rend their garments to shreds in a similar attempt, he had directed them to wait below for him, and himself securely perched upon the summit of the palisade he unslung his spear and lowered one end of it to Chulk.

The ape seized it, and while Tarzan held tightly to the upper end, the anthropoid climbed quickly up the shaft until with one paw he grasped the top of the wall. To scramble then to Tarzan's side was the work of but an instant. In like manner Taglat was conducted to their sides, and a moment later the three dropped silently within the enclosure.

Tarzan led them first to the rear of the hut in which Jane Clayton was confined, where, through the roughly repaired aperture in the wall, he sought with his sensitive nostrils for proof that the she-he had come for was within.

Chulk and Taglat, their hairy faces pressed close to that of the patrician, sniffed with him. Each caught the scent spoor of the woman within, and each reacted according to his temperament and his habits of thought.

It left Chulk indifferent. The she was for Tarzan—all that he desired was to bury his snout in the foodstuffs of the Tarmangani. He had come to eat his fill without labor—Tarzan had told him that that should be his reward, and he was satisfied.

But Taglat's wicked, bloodshot eyes, narrowed to the realization of the nearing fulfillment of his carefully nursed plan. It is true that sometimes during the several days that had

elapsed since they had set out upon their expedition it had
been difficult for Taglat to hold his idea uppermost in his
mind, and on several occasions he had completely forgotten
it, until Tarzan, by a chance word, had recalled it to him,
but, for an ape, Taglat had done well.

Now, he licked his chops, and made a sickening, sucking
noise with his flabby lips as he drew in his breath.

Satisfied that the she was where he had hoped to find her,
Tarzan led his apes toward the tent of Achmet Zek. A passing Arab and two slaves saw them, but the night was dark
and the white burnooses hid the hairy limbs of the apes and
the giant figure of their leader, so that the three, by squatting
down as though in conversation, were passed by, unsuspected.
To the rear of the tent they made their way. Within, Achmet Zek conversed with several of his lieutenants. Without,
Tarzan listened.

17

The Deadly Peril of Jane Clayton

LIEUTENANT Albert Werper, terrified by contemplation of the
fate which might await him at Adis Abeba, cast about
for some scheme of escape, but after the black Mugambi had eluded their viligance the Abyssinians redoubled
their precautions to prevent Werper following the lead of the
negro.

For some time Werper entertained the idea of bribing
Abdul Mourak with a portion of the contents of the pouch;
but fearing that the man would demand all the gems as the
price of liberty, the Belgian, influenced by avarice, sought another avenue from his dilemma.

It was then that there dawned upon him the possibility
of the success of a different course which would still leave
him in possession of the jewels, while at the same time satisfying the greed of the Abyssinian with the conviction that he
had obtained all that Werper had to offer.

And so it was that a day or so after Mugambi had disappeared, Werper asked for an audience with Abdul Mourak.
As the Belgian entered the presence of his captor the scowl
upon the features of the latter boded ill for any hope which

Werper might entertain, still he fortified himself by recalling the common weakness of mankind, which permits the most inflexible of natures to bend to the consuming desire for wealth.

Abdul Mourak eyed him, frowningly. "What do you want now?" he asked.

"My liberty," replied Werper.

The Abyssinian sneered. "And you disturbed me thus to tell me what any fool might know," he said.

"I can pay for it," said Werper.

Abdul Mourak laughed loudly. "Pay for it?" he cried. "What with—the rags that you have upon your back? Or, perhaps you are concealing beneath your coat a thousand pounds of ivory. Get out! You are a fool. Do not bother me again or I shall have you whipped."

But Werper persisted. His liberty and perhaps his life depended upon his success.

"Listen to me," he pleaded. "If I can give you as much gold as ten men may carry will you promise that I shall be conducted in safety to the nearest English commissioner?"

"As much gold as ten men may carry!" repeated Abdul Mourak. "You are crazy. Where have you so much gold as that?"

"I know where it is hid," said Werper. "Promise, and I will lead you to it—if ten loads is enough?"

Abdul Mourak had ceased to laugh. He was eyeing the Belgian intently. The fellow seemed sane enough—yet ten loads of gold! It was preposterous. The Abyssinian thought in silence for a moment.

"Well, and if I promise," he said. "How far is this gold?"

"A long week's march to the south," replied Werper.

"And if we do not find it where you say it is, do you realize what your punishment will be?"

"If it is not there I will forfeit my life," replied the Belgian. "I know it is there, for I saw it buried with my own eyes. And more—there are not only ten loads, but as many as fifty men may carry. It is all yours if you will promise to see me safely delivered into the protection of the English."

"You will stake your life against the finding of the gold?" asked Abdul.

Werper assented with a nod.

"Very well," said the Abyssinian, "I promise, and even if there be but five loads you shall have your freedom; but until the gold is in my possession you remain a prisoner."

"I am satisfied," said Werper. "Tomorrow we start?"

Abdul Mourak nodded, and the Belgian returned to his

guards. The following day the Abyssinian soldiers were surprised to receive an order which turned their faces from the
northeast to the south. And so it happened that upon the
very night that Tarzan and the two apes entered the village
of the raiders, the Abyssinians camped but a few miles to the
east of the same spot.

While Werper dreamed of freedom and the unmolested enjoyment of the fortune in his stolen pouch, and Abdul
Mourak lay awake in greedy contemplation of the fifty loads
of gold which lay but a few days farther to the south of him,
Achmet Zek gave orders to his lieutenants that they should
prepare a force of fighting men and carriers to proceed to the
ruins of the Englishman's douar on the morrow and bring
back the fabulous fortune which his renegade lieutenant had
told him was buried there.

And as he delivered his instructions to those within, a
silent listener crouched without his tent, waiting for the time
when he might enter in safety and prosecute his search for
the missing pouch and the pretty pebbles that had caught his
fancy.

At last the swarthy companions of Achmet Zek quitted his
tent, and the leader went with them to smoke a pipe with one
of their number, leaving his own silken habitation unguarded.
Scarcely had they left the interior when a knife blade was
thrust through the fabric of the rear wall, some six feet
above the ground, and a swift downward stroke opened an
entrance to those who waited beyond.

Through the opening stepped the ape-man, and close behind him came the huge Chulk; but Taglat did not follow
them. Instead he turned and slunk through the darkness toward the hut where the she who had arrested his brutish interest lay securely bound. Before the doorway the sentries
sat upon their haunches, conversing in monotones. Within,
the young woman lay upon a filthy sleeping mat, resigned,
through utter hopelessness to whatever fate lay in store for
her until the opportunity arrived which would permit her to
free herself by the only means which now seemed even re-
motely possible—the hitherto detested act of self-destruction.

Creeping silently toward the sentries, a white-burnoosed
figure approached the shadows at one end of the hut. The
meager intellect of the creature denied it the advantage it
might have taken of its disguise. Where it could have walked
boldly to the very sides of the sentries, it chose rather to
sneak upon them, unseen, from the rear.

It came to the corner of the hut and peered around.
The sentries were but a few paces away; but the ape did not
dare expose himself, even for an instant, to those feared and

hated thunder-sticks which the Tarmangani knew so well
how to use, if there were another and safer method of attack.

Taglat wished that there was a tree nearby from the overhanging branches of which he might spring upon his unsuspecting prey; but, though there was no tree, the idea gave
birth to a plan. The eaves of the hut were just above the
heads of the sentries—from them he could leap upon the
Tarmangani, unseen. A quick snap of those mighty jaws
would dispose of one of them before the other realized that
they were attacked, and the second would fall an easy prey
to the strength, agility and ferocity of a second quick charge.

Taglat withdrew a few paces to the rear of the hut, gathered himself for the effort, ran quickly forward and leaped
high into the air. He struck the roof directly above the rear
wall of the hut, and the structure, reinforced by the wall
beneath, held his enormous weight for an instant, then he
moved forward a step, the roof sagged, the thatching parted
and the great anthropoid shot through into the interior.

The sentries, hearing the crashing of the roof poles, leaped
to their feet and rushed into the hut. Jane Clayton tried to roll
aside as the great form lit upon the floor so close to her that
one foot pinned her clothing to the ground.

The ape, feeling the movement beside him, reached down
and gathered the girl in the hollow of one mighty arm. The
burnoose covered the hairy body so that Jane Clayton believed that a human arm supported her, and from the extremity of hopelessness a great hope sprang into her breast that
at last she was in the keeping of a rescuer.

The two sentries were now within the hut, but hesitating
because of doubt as to the nature of the cause of the disturbance. Their eyes, not yet accustomed to the darkness
of the interior, told them nothing, nor did they hear any
sound, for the ape stood silently awaiting their attack.

Seeing that they stood without advancing, and realizing
that, handicapped as he was by the weight of the she, he could
put up but a poor battle, Taglat elected to risk a sudden
break for liberty. Lowering his head, he charged straight for
the two sentries who blocked the doorway. The impact of his
mighty shoulders bowled them over upon their backs, and
before they could scramble to their feet, the ape was
gone, darting in the shadows of the huts toward the palisade
at the far end of the village.

The speed and strength of her rescuer filled Jane Clayton
with wonder. Could it be that Tarzan had survived the bullet
of the Arab? Who else in all the jungle could bear the weight
of a grown woman as lightly as he who held her? She spoke

his name; but there was no response. Still she did not give up hope.

At the palisade the beast did not even hesitate. A single mighty leap carried it to the top, where it poised but for an instant before dropping to the ground upon the opposite side. Now the girl was almost positive that she was safe in the arms of her husband, and when the ape took to the trees and bore her swiftly into the jungle, as Tarzan had done at other times in the past, belief became conviction.

In a little moonlit glade, a mile or so from the camp of the raiders, her rescuer halted and dropped her to the ground. His roughness surprised her, but still she had no doubts. Again she called him by name, and at the same instant the ape, fretting under the restraints of the unaccustomed garments of the Tarmangani, tore the burnoose from him, revealing to the eyes of the horror-struck woman the hideous face and hairy form of a giant anthropoid.

With a piteous wail of terror, Jane Clayton swooned, while, from the concealment of a nearby bush, Numa, the lion, eyed the pair hungrily and licked his chops.

Tarzan, entering the tent of Achmet Zek, searched the interior thoroughly. He tore the bed to pieces and scattered the contents of box and bag about the floor. He investigated whatever his eyes discovered, nor did those keen organs overlook a single article within the habitation of the raider chief; but no pouch or pretty pebbles rewarded his thoroughness.

Satisfied at last that his belongings were not in the possession of Achmet Zek, unless they were on the person of the chief himself, Tarzan decided to secure the person of the she before further prosecuting his search for the pouch.

Motioning for Chulk to follow him, he passed out of the tent by the same way that he had entered it, and walking boldly through the village, made directly for the hut where Jane Clayton had been imprisoned.

He noted with surprise the absence of Taglat, whom he had expected to find awaiting him outside the tent of Achmet Zek; but, accustomed as he was to the unreliability of apes, he gave no serious attention to the present defection of his surly companion. So long as Taglat did not cause interference with his plans, Tarzan was indifferent to his absence.

As he approached the hut, the ape-man noticed that a crowd had collected about the entrance. He could see that the men who composed it were much excited, and fearing lest Chulk's disguise should prove inadequate to the concealment of his true identity in the face of so many observers, he commanded the ape to betake himself to the far end of the village, and there await him.

As Chulk waddled off, keeping to the shadows, Tarzan advanced boldly toward the excited group before the doorway of the hut. He mingled with the blacks and the Arabs in an endeavor to learn the cause of the commotion, in his interest forgetting that he alone of the assemblage carried a spear, a bow and arrows, and thus might become an object of suspicious attention.

Shouldering his way through the crowd he approached the doorway, and had almost reached it when one of the Arabs laid a hand upon his shoulder, crying: "Who is this?" at the same time snatching back the hood from the ape-man's face.

Tarzan of the Apes in all his savage life had never been accustomed to pause in argument with an antagonist. The primitive instinct of self-preservation acknowledges many arts and wiles; but argument is not one of them, nor did he now waste precious time in an attempt to convince the raiders that he was not a wolf in sheep's clothing. Instead he had his unmasker by the throat ere the man's words had scarce quitted his lips, and hurling him from side to side brushed away those who would have swarmed upon him.

Using the Arab as a weapon, Tarzan forced his way quickly to the doorway, and a moment later was within the hut. A hasty examination revealed the fact that it was empty, and his sense of smell discovered, too, the scent spoor of Taglat, the ape. Tarzan uttered a low, ominous growl. Those who were pressing forward at the doorway to seize him, fell back as the savage notes of the bestial challenge smote upon their ears. They looked at one another in surprise and consternation. A man had entered the hut alone, and yet with their own ears they had heard the voice of a wild beast within. What could it mean? Had a lion or a leopard sought sanctuary in the interior, unbeknown to the sentries?

Tarzan's quick eyes discovered the opening in the roof, through which Taglat had fallen. He guessed that the ape had either come or gone by way of the break, and while the Arabs hesitated without, he sprang, catlike, for the opening, grasped the top of the wall and clambered out upon the roof, dropping instantly to the ground at the rear of the hut.

When the Arabs finally mustered courage to enter the hut, after firing several volleys through the walls, they found the interior deserted. At the same time Tarzan, at the far end of the village, sought for Chulk; but the ape was nowhere to be found.

Robbed of his she, deserted by his companions, and as much in ignorance as ever as to the whereabouts of his pouch and pebbles, it was an angry Tarzan who climbed the palisade and vanished into the darkness of the jungle.

For the present he must give up the search for his pouch, since it would be paramount to self-destruction to enter the Arab camp now while all its inhabitants were aroused and upon the alert.

In his escape from the village, the ape-man had lost the spoor of the fleeing Taglat, and now he circled widely through the forest in an endeavor to again pick it up.

Chulk had remained at his post until the cries and shots of the Arabs had filled his simple soul with terror, for above all things the ape folk fear the thunder-sticks of the Tarmangani; then he had clambered nimbly over the palisade, tearing his burnoose in the effort, and fled into the depths of the jungle, grumbling and scolding as he went.

Tarzan, roaming the jungle in search of the trail of Taglat and the she, traveled swiftly. In a little moonlit glade ahead of him the great ape was bending over the prostrate form of the woman Tarzan sought. The beast was tearing at the bonds that confined her ankles and wrists, pulling and gnawing upon the cords.

The course the ape-man was taking would carry him but a short distance to the right of them, and though he could not have seen them the wind was bearing down from them to him, carrying their scent spoor strongly toward him.

A moment more and Jane Clayton's safety might have been assured, even though Numa, the lion, was already gathering himself in preparation for a charge; but Fate, already all too cruel, now outdid herself—the wind veered suddenly for a few moments, the scent spoor that would have led the ape-man to the girl's side was wafted in the opposite direction; Tarzan passed within fifty yards of the tragedy that was being enacted in the glade, and the opportunity was gone beyond recall.

18

The Fight for the Treasure

IT WAS morning before Tarzan could bring himself to a realization of the possibility of failure in his quest, and even then he would only admit that success was but delayed. He would eat and sleep, and then set forth again. The jungle was wide; but wide too were the experience and cunning of Tarzan. Taglat might travel far; but Tarzan would find him in the end, though he had to search every tree in the mighty forest.

Soliloquizing thus, the ape-man followed the spoor of Bara, the deer, the unfortunate upon which he had decided to satisfy his hunger. For half an hour the trail led the ape-man toward the east along a well-marked game path, when suddenly, to the stalker's astonishment, the quarry broke into sight, racing madly back along the narrow way straight toward the hunter.

Tarzan, who had been following along the trail, leaped so quickly to the concealing verdure at the side that the deer was still unaware of the presence of an enemy in this direction, and while the animal was still some distance away, the ape-man swung into the lower branches of a tree which overhung the trail. There he crouched, a savage beast of prey, awaiting the coming of its victim.

What had frightened the deer into so frantic a retreat, Tarzan did now know—Numa, the lion, perhaps, or Sheeta, the panther; but whatsoever it was mattered little to Tarzan of the Apes—he was ready and willing to defend his kill against any other denizen of the jungle. If he were unable to do it by means of physical prowess, he had at his command another and a greater power—his shrewd intelligence.

And so, on came the running deer, straight into the jaws of death. The ape-man turned so that his back was toward the approaching animal. He poised with bent knees upon the gently swaying limb above the trail, timing with keen ears the nearing hoof beats of frightened Bara.

In a moment the victim flashed beneath the limb and at the same instant the ape-man above sprang out and down upon its back. The weight of the man's body carried the deer

to the ground. It stumbled forward once in a futile effort
to rise, and then mighty muscles dragged its head far back,
gave the neck a vicious wrench, and Bara was dead.

Quick had been the killing, and equally quick were the
ape-man's subsequent actions, for who might know what manner of killer pursued Bara, or how close at hand he might be?
Scarce had the neck of the victim snapped than the carcass
was hanging over one of Tarzan's broad shoulders, and an
instant later the ape-man was perched once more among the
lower branches of a tree above the trail, his keen, gray eyes
scanning the pathway down which the deer had fled.

Nor was it long before the cause of Bara's fright became
evident to Tarzan, for presently came the unmistakable sounds
of approaching horsemen. Dragging his kill after him the
ape-man ascended to the middle terrace, and settling himself
comfortably in the crotch of a tree where he could still view
the trail beneath, cut a juicy steak from the deer's loin, and
burying his strong, white teeth in the hot flesh proceeded to
enjoy the fruits of his prowess and his cunning.

Nor did he neglect the trail beneath while he satisfied
his hunger. His sharp eyes saw the muzzle of the leading
horse as it came into view around a bend in the tortuous
trail, and one by one they scrutinized the riders as they
passed beneath him in single file.

Among them came one whom Tarzan recognized, but so
schooled was the ape-man in the control of his emotions
that no slightest change of expression, much less any hys-
terical demonstration that might have revealed his presence,
betrayed the fact of his inward excitement.

Beneath him, as unconscious of his presence as were the
Abyssinians before and behind him, rode Albert Werper,
while the ape-man scrutinized the Belgian for some sign of
the pouch which he had stolen.

As the Abyssinians rode toward the south, a giant figure
hovered ever upon their trail—a huge, almost naked white
man, who carried the bloody carcass of a deer upon his
shoulders, for Tarzan knew that he might not have another
opportunity to hunt for some time if he were to follow the
Belgian.

To endeavor to snatch him from the midst of the armed
horsemen, not even Tarzan would attempt other than in the
last extremity, for the way of the wild is the way of caution and cunning, unless they be aroused to rashness by
pain or anger.

So the Abyssinians and the Belgian marched southward
and Tarzan of the Apes swung silently after them through
the swaying branches of the middle terrace.

A two days' march brought them to a level plain beyond which lay mountains—a plain which Tarzan remembered and which aroused within him vague half memories and strange longings. Out upon the plain the horsemen rode, and at a safe distance behind them crept the ape-man, taking advantage of such cover as the ground afforded.

Beside a charred pile of timbers the Abyssinians halted, and Tarzan, sneaking close and concealing himself in nearby shrubbery, watched them in wonderment. He saw them digging up the earth, and he wondered if they had hidden meat there in the past and now had come for it. Then he recalled how he had buried his pretty pebbles, and the suggestion that had caused him to do it. They were digging for the things the blacks had buried here!

Presently he saw them uncover a dirty, yellow object, and he witnessed the joy of Werper and of Abdul Mourak as the grimy object was exposed to view. One by one they unearthed many similar pieces, all of the same uniform, dirty yellow, until a pile of them lay upon the ground, a pile which Abdul Mourak fondled and petted in an ecstasy of greed.

Something stirred in the ape-man's mind as he looked long upon the golden ingots. Where had he seen such before? What were they? Why did these Tarmangani covet them so greatly? To whom did they belong?

He recalled the black men who had buried them. The things must be theirs. Werper was stealing them as he had stolen Tarzan's pouch of pebbles. The ape-man's eyes blazed in anger. He would like to find the black men and lead them against these thieves. He wondered where their village might be.

As all these things ran through the active mind, a party of men moved out of the forest at the edge of the plain and advanced toward the ruins of the burned bungalow.

Abdul Mourak, always watchful, was the first to see them, but already they were halfway across the open. He called to his men to mount and hold themselves in readiness, for in the heart of Africa who may know whether a strange host be friend or foe?

Werper, swinging into his saddle, fastened his eyes upon the newcomers, then, white and trembling he turned toward Abdul Mourak.

"It is Achmet Zek and his raiders," he whispered. "They are come for the gold."

It must have been at about the same instant that Achmet Zek discovered the pile of yellow ingots and realized the actuality of what he had already feared since first his eyes had alighted upon the party beside the ruins of the English-man's bungalow. Someone had forestalled him—another had come for the treasure ahead of him.

The Arab was crazed by rage. Recently everything had gone against him. He had lost the jewels, the Belgian, and for the second time he had lost the Englishwoman. Now some one had come to rob him of this treasure which he had thought as safe from disturbance here as though it never had been mined.

He cared not whom the thieves might be. They would not give up the gold without a battle, of that he was certain, and with a wild whoop and a command to his followers, Achmet Zek put spurs to his horse and dashed down upon the Abyssinians, and after him, waving their long guns above their heads, yelling and cursing, came his motley horde of cut-throat followers.

The men of Abdul Mourak met them with a volley which emptied a few saddles, and then the raiders were among them, and sword, pistol and musket, each was doing its most hideous and bloody work.

Achmet Zek, spying Werper at the first charge, bore down upon the Belgian, and the latter, terrified by contempla-tion of the fate he deserved, turned his horse's head and dashed madly away in an effort to escape. Shouting to a lieutenant to take command, and urging him upon pain of death to dispatch the Abyssinians and bring the gold back to his camp, Achmet Zek set off across the plain in pursuit of the Belgian, his wicked nature unable to forego the pleasures of revenge, even at the risk of sacrificing the treasure.

As the pursued and the pursuer raced madly toward the distant forest the battle behind them raged with bloody savageness. No quarter was asked or given by either the ferocious Abyssinians or the murderous cut-throats of Achmet Zek.

From the concealment of the shrubbery Tarzan watched the sanguinary conflict which so effectually surrounded him that he found no loop-hole through which he might escape to follow Werper and the Arab chief.

The Abyssinians were formed in a circle which in-cluded Tarzan's position, and around and into them gal-loped the yelling raiders, now darting away, now charging in to deliver thrusts and cuts with their curved swords.

Numerically the men of Achmet Zek were superior, and slowly but surely the soldiers of Menelek were being ex-terminated. To Tarzan the result was immaterial. He watched with but a single purpose—to escape the ring of blood-mad fighters and be away after the Belgian and his pouch.

When he had first discovered Werper upon the trail where he had slain Bara, he had thought that his eyes must be playing him false, so certain had he been that the thief had been slain and devoured by Numa; but after following the detachment for two days, with his keen eyes always upon the Belgian, he no longer doubted the identity of the man, though he was put to it to explain the identity of the mutilated corpse he had supposed was the man he sought.

As he crouched in hiding among the unkempt shrubbery which so short a while since had been the delight and pride of the wife he no longer recalled, an Arab and an Abyssinian wheeled their mounts close to his position as they slashed at each other with their swords.

Step by step the Arab beat back his adversary until the latter's horse all but trod upon the ape-man, and then a vicious cut clove the black warrior's skull, and the corpse toppled backward almost upon Tarzan.

As the Abyssinian tumbled from his saddle the possibility of escape which was represented by the riderless horse electrified the ape-man to instant action. Before the frightened beast could gather himself for flight a naked giant was astride his back. A strong hand had grasped his bridle rein, and the surprised Arab discovered a new foe in the saddle of him, whom he had slain.

But this enemy wielded no sword, and his spear and bow remained upon his back. The Arab, recovered from his first surprise, dashed in with raised sword to annihilate this presumptious stranger. He aimed a mighty blow at the ape-man's head, a blow which swung harmlessly through thin air as Tarzan ducked from its path, and then the Arab felt the other's horse brushing his leg, a great arm shot out and encircled his waist, and before he could recover himself he was dragged from his saddle, and forming a shield for his antagonist was borne at a mad run straight through the encircling ranks of his fellows.

Just beyond them he was tossed aside upon the ground, and the last he saw of his strange foeman the latter was galloping off across the plain in the direction of the forest at its farther edge.

For another hour the battle raged nor did it cease until the last of the Abyssinians lay dead upon the ground, or had galloped off toward the north in flight. But a handful of men escaped, among them Abdul Mourak.

The victorious raiders collected about the pile of golden ingots which the Abyssinians had uncovered, and there awaited the return of their leader. Their exultation was slightly tempered by the glimpse they had had of the strange apparition of the naked white man galloping away upon the horse of one of their foemen and carrying a companion who was now among them expatiating upon the superhuman strength of the ape-man. None of them there but was familiar with the name and fame of Tarzan of the Apes, and the fact that they had recognized the white giant as the ferocious enemy of the wrongdoers of the jungle, added to their terror, for they had been assured that Tarzan was dead.

Naturally superstitious, they fully believed that they had seen the disembodied spirit of the dead man, and now they cast fearful glances about them in expectation of the ghost's early return to the scene of the ruin they had inflicted upon him during their recent raid upon his home, and discussed in affrighted whispers the probable nature of the vengeance which the spirit would inflict upon them should he return to find them in possession of his gold.

As they conversed their terror grew, while from the concealment of the reeds along the river below them a small party of naked, black warriors watched their every move. From the heights beyond the river these black men had heard the noise of the conflict, and creeping warily down to the stream had forded it and advanced through the reeds until they were in a position to watch every move of the combatants.

For a half hour the raiders awaited Achmet Zek's return, their fear of the earlier return of the ghost of Tarzan constantly undermining their loyalty to and fear of their chief. Finally one among them voiced the desires of all when he announced that he intended riding forth toward the forest in search of Achmet Zek. Instantly every man of them sprang to his mount.

"The gold will be safe here," cried one. "We have killed the Abyssinians and there are no others to carry it away. Let us ride in search of Achmet Zek!"

And a moment later, amidst a cloud of dust, the raiders were galloping madly across the plain, and out from the concealment of the reeds along the river, crept a party of black warriors toward the spot where the golden ingots of Opar lay piled on the ground.

Werper had still been in advance of Achmet Zek when he reached the forest; but the latter, better mounted, was gaining upon him. Riding with the reckless courage of desperation the Belgian urged his mount to greater speed even within the narrow confines of the winding, game trail that the beast was following.

Behind him he could hear the voice of Achmet Zek crying to him to halt; but Werper only dug the spurs deeper into the bleeding sides of his panting mount. Two hundred yards within the forest a broken branch lay across the trail. It was a small thing that a horse might ordinarily take in his natural stride without noticing its presence; but Werper's horse was jaded, his feet were heavy with weariness, and as the branch caught between his front legs he stumbled, was unable to recover himself, and went down, sprawling in the trail.

Werper, going over his head rolled a few yards farther on, scrambled to his feet and ran back. Seizing the reins he tugged to drag the beast to his feet; but the animal would not or could not rise, and as the Belgian cursed and struck at him, Achmet Zek appeared in view.

Instantly the Belgian ceased his efforts with the dying animal at his feet, and seizing his rifle, dropped behind the horse and fired at the oncoming Arab.

His bullet, going low, struck Achmet Zek's horse in the breast, bringing him down a hundred yards from where Werper lay preparing to fire a second shot.

The Arab, who had gone down with his mount, was standing astride him, and seeing the Belgian's strategic position behind his fallen horse, lost no time in taking up a similar one behind his own.

And there the two lay, alternately firing at and cursing each other, while from behind the Arab, Tarzan of the Apes approached to the edge of the forest. Here he heard the occasional shots of the duelists, and choosing the safer and swifter avenue of the forest branches to the uncertain transportation afforded by a half-broken Abyssinian pony, took to the trees.

Keeping to one side of the trail, the ape-man came presently to a point where he could look down in comparative safety upon the fighters. First one and then the other would partially raise himself above his breastwork of horseflesh, fire his weapon and immediately drop flat behind his shelter, where he would reload and repeat the act a moment later.

Werper had but little ammunition, having been hastily armed by Abdul Mourak from the body of one of the first of the Abyssinians who had fallen in the fight about the pile of ingots, and now he realized that soon he would have used his last bullet, and be at the mercy of the Arab— a mercy with which he was well acquainted.

Facing both death and despoilment of his treasure, the Belgian cast about for some plan of escape, and the only one that appealed to him as containing even a remote possibility of success hinged upon the chance of bribing Achmet Zek.

Werper had fired all but a single cartridge, when, during a lull in the fighting, he called aloud to his opponent.

"Achmet Zek," he cried, "Allah alone know which one of us may leave our bones to rot where he lies upon this trail today if we keep up our foolish battle. You wish the contents of the pouch I wear about my waist, and I wish my life and my liberty even more than I do the jewels. Let us each, then, take that which he most desires and go our separate ways in peace. I will lay the pouch upon the carcass of my horse, where you may see it, and you, in turn, will lay your gun upon your horse, with butt toward me. Then I will go away, leaving the pouch to you, and you will let me go in safety. I want only my life, and my freedom."

The Arab thought in silence for a moment. Then he spoke. His reply was influenced by the fact that he had expended his last shot.

"Go your way, then," he growled, "leaving the pouch in plain sight behind you. See, I lay my gun thus, with the butt toward you. Go."

Werper removed the pouch from about his waist. Sorrowfully and affectionately he let his fingers press the hard outlines of the contents. Ah, if he could but extract a little handful of the precious stones! But Achmet Zek was standing now, his eagle eyes commanding a plain view of the Belgian had his every act.

Regretfully Werper laid the pouch, its contents undisturbed, upon the body of his horse, rose, and taking his rifle with him, backed slowly down the trail until a turn hid him from the view of the watchful Arab.

Even then Achmet Zek did not advance, fearful as he was of some such treachery as he himself might have been guilty of under like circumstances; nor were his suspicions groundless, for the Belgian, no sooner had he passed out of the range of the Arab's vision, halted behind the bole of a tree, where he still commanded an unobstructed view of his dead horse and the pouch, and raising his rifle covered the spot where the other's body must appear when he came forward to seize the treasure.

But Achmet Zek was no fool to expose himself to the blackened honor of a thief and a murderer. Taking his long gun with him, he left the trail, entering the rank and tangled vegetation which walled it, and crawling slowly forward on hands and knees he paralleled the trail; but never for an instant was his body exposed to the rifle of the hidden assassin.

Thus Achmet Zek advanced until he had come opposite the dead horse of his enemy. The pouch lay there in full view, while a short distance along the trail, Werper waited in growing impatience and nervousness, wondering why the Arab did not come to claim his reward.

Presently he saw the muzzle of a rifle appear suddenly and mysteriously a few inches above the pouch, and before he could realize the cunning trick that the Arab had played upon him the sight of the weapon was adroitly hooked into the rawhide thong which formed the carrying strap of the pouch, and the latter was drawn quickly from his view into the dense foliage at the trail's side.

Not for an instant had the raider exposed a square inch of his body, and Werper dared not fire his one remaining shot unless every chance of a successful hit was in his favor.

Chuckling to himself, Achmet Zek withdrew a few paces farther into the jungle, for he was as positive that Werper was waiting nearby for a chance to pot him as though his eyes had penetrated the jungle trees to the figure of the hiding Belgian, fingering his rifle behind the bole of the buttressed giant.

Werper did not dare advance—his cupidity would not permit him to depart, and so he stood there, his rifle ready in his hands, his eyes watching the trail before him with cat-like intensity.

But there was another who had seen the pouch and recognized it, who did advance with Achmet Zek, hovering above him, as silent and as sure as death itself, and as the Arab, finding a little spot less overgrown with bushes than he had yet encountered, prepared to gloat his eyes upon the contents of the pouch, Tarzan paused directly above him, intent upon the same object.

Wetting his thin lips with his tongue, Achmet Zek loosened the tie strings which closed the mouth of the pouch, and cupping one claw-like hand poured forth a portion of the contents into his palm.

A single look he took at the stones lying in his hand. His eyes narrowed, a curse broke from his lips, and he hurled the small objects upon the ground, disdainfully. Quickly he emptied the balance of the contents until he had scanned each separate stone, and as he dumped them all upon the ground and stamped upon them his rage grew until the muscles of his face worked in demon-like fury, and his fingers clenched until his nails bit into the flesh.

Above, Tarzan watched in wonderment. He had been curious to discover what all the pow-wow about his pouch had meant. He wanted to see what the Arab would do after the other had gone away, leaving the pouch behind him, and, having satisfied his curiosity, he would then have pounced upon Achmet Zek and taken the pouch and his pretty pebbles away from him, for did they not belong to Tarzan?

He saw the Arab now throw aside the empty pouch, and grasping his long gun by the barrel, clublike, sneak stealthily through the jungle beside the trail along which Werper had gone.

As the man disappeared from his view, Tarzan dropped to the ground and commenced gathering up the spilled contents of the pouch, and the moment that he obtained his first near view of the scattered pebbles he understood the rage of the Arab, for instead of the glittering and scintillating gems which had first caught and held the attention of the ape-man, the pouch had now contained but a collection of ordinary river pebbles.

19

Jane Clayton and the Beasts of the Jungle

MUGAMBI, after his successful break for liberty, had fallen upon hard times. His way had led him through a country with which he was unfamiliar, a jungle country in which he could find no water, and but little food, so that after several days of wandering he found himself so reduced in strength that he could barely drag himself along.

It was with growing difficulty that he found the strength necessary to construct a shelter by night wherein he might be reasonably safe from the large carnivora, and by day he still further exhausted his strength in digging for edible roots, and searching for water.

A few stagnant pools at considerable distances apart saved him from death by thirst; but his was a pitiable state when finally he stumbled by accident upon a large river in a country where fruit was abundant, and small game which he might bag by means of a combination of stealth, cunning, and a crude knob-stick which he had fashioned from a fallen limb.

Realizing that he still had a long march ahead of him

before he could reach even the outskirts of the Waziri country, Mugambi wisely decided to remain where he was until he had recuperated his strength and health. A few days' rest would accomplish wonders for him, he knew, and he could ill afford to sacrifice his chances for a safe return by setting forth handicapped by weakness.

And so it was that he constructed a substantial thorn boma, and rigged a thatched shelter within it, where he might sleep by night in security, and from which he sallied forth by day to hunt the flesh which alone could return to his giant thews their normal prowess.

One day, as he hunted, a pair of savage eyes discovered him from the concealment of the branches of a great tree beneath which the black warrior passed. Bloodshot, wicked eyes they were, set in a fierce and hairy face.

They watched Mugambi make his little kill of a small rodent, and they followed him as he returned to his hut, their owner moving quietly through the trees upon the trail of the negro.

The creature was Chulk, and he looked down upon the unconscious man more in curiosity than in hate. The wearing of the Arab burnoose which Tarzan had placed upon his person had aroused in the mind of the anthropoid a desire for similar mimicry of the Tarmangani. The burnoose, though, had obstructed his movements and proven such a nuisance that the ape had long since torn it from him and thrown it away.

Now, however, he saw a Gomangani arrayed in less cumbersome apparel—a loin cloth, a few copper ornaments and a feather headdress. These were more in line with Chulk's desires than a flowing robe which was constantly getting between ones legs, and catching upon every limb and bush along the leafy trail.

Chulk eyed the pouch, which, suspended over Mugambi's shoulder, swung beside his black hip. This took his fancy, for it was ornamented with feathers and a fringe, and so the ape hung about Mugambi's boma, waiting an opportunity to seize either by stealth or might some object of the black's apparel.

Nor was it long before the opportunity came. Feeling safe within his thorny enclosure, Mugambi was wont to stretch himself in the shade of his shelter during the heat of the day, and sleep in peaceful security until the declining sun carried with it the enervating temperature of midday.

Watching from above, Chulk saw the black warrior stretched thus in the unconsciousness of sleep one sultry afternoon. Creeping out upon an overhanging branch the anthropoid dropped to the ground within the boma. He approached the sleeper upon padded feet which gave forth no sound, and with an uncanny woodcraft that rustled not a leaf or a grass blade.

Pausing beside the man, the ape bent over and examined his belongings. Great as was the strength of Chulk there lay in the back of his little brain a something which deterred him from arousing the man to combat—a sense that is inherent in all of the lower orders, a strange fear of man, that rules even the most powerful of the jungle creatures at times.

To remove Mugambi's loin cloth without awakening him would be impossible, and the only detachable things were the knob-stick and the pouch, which had fallen from the black's shoulder as he rolled in sleep.

Seizing these two articles, as better than nothing at all, Chulk retreated with haste, and every indication of nervous terror, to the safety of the tree from which he had dropped, and, still haunted by that indefinable terror which the close proximity of man awakened in his breast, fled precipitately through the jungle. Aroused by attack, or supported by the presence of another of his kind, Chulk could have braved the presence of a score of human beings, but alone—ah, that was a different matter—alone, and unenraged.

It was some time after Mugambi awoke that he missed the pouch. Instantly he was all excitement. What could have become of it? It had been at his side when he lay down to sleep—of that he was certain, for had he not pushed it from beneath him when its bulging bulk, pressing against his ribs, caused him discomfort? Yes, it had been there when he lay down to sleep. How then had it vanished?

Mugambi's savage imagination was filled with visions of the spirits of departed friends and enemies, for only to the machinations of such as these could he attribute the disappearance of his pouch and knob-stick in the first excitement of the discovery of their loss; but later and more careful investigation, such as his woodcraft made possible, revealed indisputable evidence of a more material explanation than his excited fancy and superstition had at first led him to accept.

In the trampled turf beside him was the faint impress of huge, manlike feet. Mugambi raised his brows as the truth dawned upon him. Hastily leaving the boma he searched in all directions about the enclosure for some further sign of the tell-tale spoor. He climbed trees and sought for evidence of the direction of the thief's flight; but the faint signs left by a wary ape who elects to travel through the trees eluded the woodcraft of Mugambi. Tarzan might have followed them;

but no ordinary mortal could perceive them, or perceiving, translate.

The black, now strengthened and refreshed by his rest, felt ready to set out again for Waziri, and finding himself another knob-stick, turned his back upon the river and plunged into the mazes of the jungle.

As Taglat struggled with the bonds which secured the ankles and wrists of his captive, the great lion that eyed the two from behind a nearby clump of bushes wormed closer to his intended prey.

The ape's back was toward the lion. He did not see the broad head, fringed by its rough mane, protruding through the leafy wall. He could not know that the powerful hind paws were gathering close beneath the tawny belly preparatory to a sudden spring, and his first intimation of impending danger was the thunderous and triumphant roar which the charging lion could no longer suppress.

Scarce pausing for a backward glance, Taglat abandoned the unconscious woman and fled in the opposite direction from the horrid sound which had broken in so unexpected and terrifying a manner upon his startled ears; but the warning had come too late to save him, and the lion, in his second bound, alighted full upon the broad shoulders of the anthropoid.

As the great bull went down there was awakened in him to the full all the cunning, all the ferocity, all the physical prowess which obey the mightiest of the fundamental laws of nature, the law of self-preservation, and turning upon his back he closed with the carnivore in a death struggle so fearless and abandoned, that for a moment the great Numa himself may have trembled for the outcome.

Seizing the lion by the mane, Taglat buried his yellowed fangs deep in the monster's throat, growling hideously through the muffled gag of blood and hair. Mixed with the ape's voice the lion's roars of rage and pain reverberated through the jungle, till the lesser creatures of the wild, startled from their peaceful pursuits, scurried fearfully away.

Rolling over and over upon the turf the two battled with demoniac fury, until the colossal cat, by doubling his hind paws far up beneath his belly sank his talons deep into Taglat's chest, then, ripping downward with all his strength, Numa accomplished his design, and the disemboweled anthropoid, with a last spasmodic struggle, relaxed in limp and bloody disolution beneath his titanic adversary.

Scrambling to his feet, Numa looked about quickly in all directions, as though seeking to detect the possible presence of other foes; but only the still and unconscious form of the girl, lying a few paces from him met his gaze, and with an angry growl he placed a forepaw upon the body of his kill and raising his head gave voice to his savage victory cry.

For another moment he stood with fierce eyes roving to and fro about the clearing. At last they halted for a second time upon the girl. A low growl rumbled from the lion's throat. His lower jaw rose and fell, and the slaver drooled and dripped upon the dead face of Taglat.

Like two yellow-green augurs, wide and unblinking, the terrible eyes remained fixed upon Jane Clayton. The erect and majestic pose of the great frame shrank suddenly into a sinister crouch as, slowly and gently as one who treads on eggs, the devil-faced cat crept forward toward the girl.

Beneficent Fate maintained her in happy unconsciousness of the dread presence sneaking stealthily upon her. She did not know when the lion paused at her side. She did not hear the sniffing of his nostrils as he smelled about her. She did not feel the heat of the fetid breath upon her face, nor the dripping of the saliva from the frightful jaws half opened so close above her.

Finally the lion lifted a forepaw and turned the body of the girl half over, then he stood again eyeing her as though still undetermined whether life was extinct or not. Some noise or odor from the nearby jungle attracted his attention for a moment. His eyes did not again return to Jane Clayton, and presently he left her, walked over to the remains of Taglat, and crouching down upon his kill with his back toward the girl, proceeded to devour the ape.

It was upon this scene that Jane Clayton at last opened her eyes. Inured to danger, she maintained her self-possession in the face of the startling surprise which her new-found consciousness revealed to her. She neither cried out nor moved a muscle, until she had taken in every detail of the scene which lay within the range of her vision.

She saw that the lion had killed the ape, and that he was devouring his prey less than fifty feet from where she lay; but what could she do? Her hands and feet were bound. She must wait then, in what patience she could command, until Numa had eaten and digested the ape, when, without doubt, he would return to feast upon her, unless, in the meantime, the dread hyenas should discover her, or some other of the numerous prowling carnivora of the jungle.

As she lay tormented by these frightful thoughts she suddenly became conscious that the bonds at her wrists and ankles no longer hurt her, and then of the fact that her hands were separated, one lying upon either side of her, instead of both being confined at her back.

Wonderingly she moved a hand. What miracle had been performed? It was not bound! Stealthily and noiselessly she moved her other limbs, only to discover that she was free. She could not know how the thing had happened, that Taglat, gnawing upon them for sinister purposes of his own, had cut them through but an instant before Numa had frightened him from his victim.

For a moment Jane Clayton was overwhelmed with joy and thanksgiving; but only for a moment. What good was her new-found liberty in the face of the frightful beast crouching so close beside her? If she could have had this chance under different conditions, how happily she would have taken advantage of it; but now it was given to her when escape was practically impossible.

The nearest tree was a hundred feet away, the lion less than fifty. To rise and attempt to reach the safety of those tantalizing branches would be but to invite instant destruction, for Numa would doubtless be too jealous of this future meal to permit it to escape with ease. And yet, too, there was another possibility—a chance which hinged entirely upon the unknown temper of the great beast.

His belly already partially filled, he might watch with indifference the departure of the girl; yet could she afford to chance so improbable a contingency? She doubted it. Upon the other hand she was no more minded to allow this frail opportunity for life to entirely elude her without taking or attempting to take some advantage from it.

She watched the lion narrowly. He could not see her without turning his head more than halfway around. She would attempt a ruse. Silently she rolled over in the direction of the nearest tree, and away from the lion, until she lay again in the same position in which Numa had left her, but a few feet farther from him.

Here she lay breathless watching the lion; but the beast gave no indication that he had heard aught to arouse his suspicions. Again she rolled over, gaining a few more feet and again she lay in rigid contemplation of the beast's back.

During what seemed hours to her tense nerves, Jane Clayton continued these tactics, and still the lion fed on in apparent unconsciousness that his second prey was escaping him. Already the girl was but a few paces from the tree—a moment more and she would be close enough to chance springing to her feet, throwing caution aside and making a sudden, bold dash for safety. She was halfway over in her turn, her face away from the lion, when he suddenly turned his great head and fastened his eyes upon her. He saw her roll over upon her side away from him, and then her eyes were turned again toward him, and the cold sweat broke from the girl's every pore as she realized that with life almost within her grasp, death had found her out.

For a long time neither the girl nor the lion moved. The beast lay motionless, his head turned upon his shoulders and his glaring eyes fixed upon the rigid victim, now nearly fifty yards away. The girl stared back straight into those cruel orbs, daring not to move even a muscle.

The strain upon her nerves was becoming so unbearable that she could scarcely restrain a growing desire to scream, when Numa deliberately turned back to the business of feeding; but his back-layed ears attested a sinister regard for the actions of the girl behind him.

Realizing that she could not again turn without attracting his immediate and perhaps fatal attention, Jane Clayton resolved to risk all in one last attempt to reach the tree and clamber to the lower branches.

Gathering herself stealthily for the effort, she leaped suddenly to her feet, but almost simultaneously the lion sprang up, wheeled and with wide-distended jaws and terrific roars, charged swiftly down upon her.

Those who have spent lifetimes hunting the big game of Africa will tell you that scarcely any other creature in the world attains the speed of a charging lion. For the short distance that the great cat can maintain it, it resembles nothing more closely than the onrushing of a giant locomotive under full speed, and so, though the distance that Jane Clayton must cover was relatively small, the terrific speed of the lion rendered her hopes of escape almost negligible.

Yet fear can work wonders, and though the upward spring of the lion as he neared the tree into which she was scrambling brought his talons in contact with her boots she eluded his raking grasp, and as he hurtled against the bole of her sanctuary, the girl drew herself into the safety of the branches above his reach.

For some time the lion paced, growling and moaning, beneath the tree in which Jane Clayton crouched, panting and trembling. The girl was a prey to the nervous reaction from the frightful ordeal through which she had so recently passed, and in her overwrought state it seemed that never again should she dare descend to the ground among the fearsome dangers which infested the broad stretch of jungle that she knew must lie between herself and the nearest village of her faithful Waziri.

It was almost dark before the lion finally quit the clearing, and even had his place beside the remnants of the mangled ape not been immediately usurped by a pack of hyenas, Jane

Clayton would scarcely have dared venture from her refuge in the face of impending night, and so she composed herself as best she could for the long and tiresome wait, until daylight might offer some means of escape from the dread vicinity in which she had witnessed such terrifying adventures.

Tired nature at last overcame even her fears, and she dropped into a deep slumber, cradled in a comparatively safe, though rather uncomfortable, position against the bole of the tree, and supported by two large branches which grew outward, almost horizontally, but a few inches apart.

The sun was high in the heavens when she at last awoke, and beneath her was no sign either of Numa or the hyenas. Only the clean-picked bones of the ape, scattered about the ground, attested the fact of what had transpired in this seemingly peaceful spot but a few hours before.

Both hunger and thirst assailed her now, and realizing that she must descend or die of starvation, she at last summoned courage to undertake the ordeal of continuing her journey through the jungle.

Descending from the tree, she set out in a southerly direction, toward the point where she believed the plains of Waziri lay, and though she knew that only ruin and desolation marked the spot where once her happy home had stood, she hoped that by coming to the broad plain she might eventually reach one of the numerous Waziri villages that were scattered over the surrounding country, or chance upon a roving band of these indefatigable huntsmen.

The day was half spent when there broke unexpectedly upon her startled ears the sound of a rifle shot not far ahead of her. As she paused to listen, this first shot was followed by another and another and another. What could it mean? The first explanation which sprung to her mind attributed the firing to an encounter between the Arab raiders and a party of Waziri; but as she did not know upon which side victory might rest, or whether she were behind friend or foe, she dared not advance nearer on the chance of revealing herself to an enemy.

After listening for several minutes she became convinced that no more than two or three rifles were engaged in the fight, since nothing approximating the sound of a volley reached her ears; but still she hesitated to approach, and at last, determining to take no chance, she climbed into the concealing foliage of a tree beside the trail she had been following and there fearfully awaited whatever might reveal itself.

As the firing became less rapid she caught the sound of men's voices, though she could distinguish no words, and at last the reports of the guns ceased, and she heard two men calling to each other in loud tones. Then there was a long silence which was finally broken by the stealthy padding of footfalls on the trail ahead of her, and in another moment a man appeared in view backing toward her, a rifle ready in his hands, and his eyes directed in careful watchfulness along the way that he had come.

Almost instantly Jane Clayton recognized the man as M. Jules Frecoult, who so recently had been a guest in her home. She was upon the point of calling to him in glad relief when she saw him leap quickly to one side and hide himself in the thick verdure at the trail's side. It was evident that he was being followed by an enemy, and so Jane Clayton kept silence, lest she distract Frecoult's attention, or guide his foe to his hiding place.

Scarcely had Frecoult hidden himself than the figure of a white-robed Arab crept silently along the trail in pursuit. From her hiding place, Jane Clayton could see both men plainly. She recognized Achmet Zek as the leader of the band of ruffians who had raided her home and made her a prisoner, and as she saw Frecoult, the supposed friend and ally, raise his gun and take careful aim at the Arab, her heart stood still and every power of her soul was directed upon a fervent prayer for the accuracy of his aim.

Achmet Zek paused in the middle of the trail. His keen eyes scanned every bush and tree within the radius of his vision. His tall figure presented a perfect target to the perfidious assassin. There was a sharp report, and a little puff of smoke arose from the bush that hid the Belgian, as Achmet Zek stumbled forward and pitched, face down, upon the trail.

As Werper stepped back into the trail, he was startled by the sound of a glad cry from above him, and as he wheeled about to discover the author of this unexpected interruption, he saw Jane Clayton drop lightly from a nearby tree and run forward with outstretched hands to congratulate him upon his victory.

20

Jane Clayton Again a Prisoner

T HOUGH her clothes were torn and her hair disheveled, Albert Werper realized that he never before had looked upon such a vision of loveliness as that which Lady Greystoke presented in the relief and joy which she felt in coming so unexpectedly upon a friend and rescuer when hope had seemed so far away.

If the Belgian had entertained any doubts as to the woman's knowledge of his part in the perfidious attack upon her home and herself, it was quickly dissipated by the genuine friendliness of her greeting. She told him quickly of all that had befallen her since he had departed from her home, and as she spoke of the death of her husband her eyes were veiled by the tears which she could not repress.

"I am shocked," said Werper, in well-simulated sympathy; "but I am not surprised. That devil there," and he pointed toward the body of Achmet Zek, "has terrorized the entire country. Your Waziri are either exterminated, or have been driven out of their country, far to the south. The men of Achmet Zek occupy the plain about your former home—there is neither sanctuary nor escape in that direction. Our only hope lies in traveling northward as rapidly as we may, of coming to the camp of the raiders before the knowledge of Achmet Zek's death reaches those who were left there, and of obtaining, through some ruse, an escort toward the north.

"I think that the thing can be accomplished, for I was a guest of the raider's before I knew the nature of the man, and those at the camp are not aware that I turned against him when I discovered his villainy.

"Come! We will make all possible haste to reach the camp before those who accompanied Achmet Zek upon his last raid have found his body and carried the news of his death to the cut-throats who remained behind. It is our only hope, Lady Greystoke, and you must place your entire faith in me if I am to succeed. Wait for me here a moment while I take from the Arab's body the wallet that he stole from me," and Werper stepped quickly to the dead man's side, and, kneeling, sought with quick fingers the pouch of jewels. To his consternation, there was no sign of them in the garments of Achmet Zek. Rising, he walked back along the trail, searching for some trace of the missing pouch or its contents; but he found nothing, even though he searched carefully the vicinity of his dead horse, and for a few paces into the jungle on either side. Puzzled, disappointed and angry, he at last returned to the girl. "The wallet is gone," he explained, crisply, "and I dare not delay longer in search of it. We must reach the camp before the returning raiders."

Unsuspicious of the man's true character, Jane Clayton saw nothing peculiar in his plans, or in his specious explanation of his former friendship for the raider, and so she grasped with alacrity the seeming hope for safety which he proffered her, and turning about she set out with Albert Werper toward the hostile camp in which she so lately had been a prisoner.

It was late in the afternoon of the second day before they reached their destination, and as they paused upon the edge of the clearing before the gates of the walled village, Werper cautioned the girl to accede to whatever he might suggest by his conversation with the raiders.

"I shall tell them," he said, "that I apprehended you after you escaped from the camp, that I took you to Achmet Zek, and that as she was engaged in a stubborn battle with the Waziri, he directed me to return to camp with you, to obtain here a sufficient guard, and to ride north with you as rapidly as possible and dispose of you at the most advantageous terms to a certain slave broker whose name he gave me."

Again the girl was deceived by the apparent frankness of the Belgian. She realized that desperate situations required desperate handling, and though she trembled inwardly at the thought of again entering the vile and hideous village of the raiders she saw no better course than that which her companion had suggested.

Calling aloud to those who tended the gates, Werper, grasping Jane Clayton by the arm, walked boldly across the clearing. Those who opened the gates to him permitted their surprise to show clearly in their expressions. That the discredited and hunted lieutenant should be thus returning fearlessly of his own volition, seemed to disarm them quite as effectually as his manner toward Lady Greystoke had deceived her.

The sentries at the gate returned Werper's salutations, and viewed with astonishment the prisoner whom he brought into the village with him.

Immediately the Belgian sought the Arab who had been left in charge of the camp during Achmet Zek's absence, and again his boldness disarmed suspicion and won the acceptance of his false explanation of his return. The fact that he had brought back with him the woman prisoner who had escaped, added strength to his claims, and Mohammed Beyd soon found himself fraternizing good-naturedly with the very man whom he would have slain without compunction had he discovered him alone in the jungle a half hour before.

Jane Clayton was again confined to the prison hut she had formerly occupied, but as she realized that this was but a part of the deception which she and Frecoult were playing upon the credulous raiders, it was with quite a different sensation that she again entered the vile and filthy interior, from that which she had previously experienced, when hope was so far away.

Once more she was bound and sentries placed before the door of her prison; but before Werper left her he whispered words of cheer into her ear. Then he left, and made his way back to the tent of Mohammed Beyd. He had been wondering how long it would be before the raiders who had ridden out with Achmet Zek would return with the murdered body of their chief, and the more he thought upon the matter the greater his fears became, that without accomplices his plan would fail.

What, even, if he got away from the camp in safety before any returned with the true story of his guilt—of what value would this advantage be other than to protract for a few days his mental torture and his life? These hard riders, familiar with every trail and bypath, would get him long before he could hope to reach the coast.

As these thoughts passed through his mind he entered the tent where Mohammed Beyd sat cross-legged upon a rug, smoking. The Arab looked up as the European came into his presence.

"Greetings, O, Brother!" he said.

"Greetings!" replied Werper.

For a while neither spoke further. The Arab was the first to break the silence.

"And my master, Achmet Zek, was well when last you saw him?" he asked.

"Never was he safer from the sins and dangers of mortality," replied the Belgian.

"It is well," said Mohammed Beyd, blowing a little puff of blue smoke straight out before him.

Again there was silence for several minutes.

"And if he were dead?" asked the Belgian, determined to lead up to the truth, and attempt to bribe Mohammed Beyd into his service.

The Arab's eyes narrowed and he leaned forward, his gaze boring straight into the eyes of the Belgian.

"I have been thinking much, Werper, since you returned so unexpectedly to the camp of the man whom you had deceived, and who sought you with death in his heart. I have been with Achmet Zek for many years—his own mother never knew him so well as I. He never forgives—much less would he again trust a man who had once betrayed him; that I know.

"I have thought much, as I said, and the result of my thinking has assured me that Achmet Zek is dead—for otherwise you would never have dared return to his camp, unless you be either a braver man or a bigger fool than I have imagined. And, if this evidence of my judgment is not sufficient, I have but just now received from your own lips even more confirmatory witness—for did you not say that Achmet Zek was never more safe from the sins and dangers of mortality?

"Achmet Zek is dead—you need not deny it. I was not his mother, or his mistress, so do not fear that my wailings shall disturb you. Tell me why you have come back here. Tell me what you want, and, Werper, if you still possess the jewels of which Achmet Zek told me, there is no reason why you and I should not ride north together and divide the ransom of the white woman and the contents of the pouch you wear about your person. Eh?"

The evil eyes narrowed, a vicious, thin-lipped smile tortured the villainous face, as Mohammed Beyd grinned knowingly into the face of the Belgian.

Werper was both relieved and disturbed by the Arab's attitude. The complacency with which he accepted the death of his chief lifted a considerable burden of apprehension from the shoulders of Achmet Zek's assassin; but his demand for a share of the jewels boded ill for Werper when Mohammed Beyd should have learned that the precious stones were no longer in the Belgian's possession.

To acknowledge that he had lost the jewels might be to arouse the wrath or suspicion of the Arab to such an extent as would jeopardize his new-found chances of escape. His one hope seemed, then, to lie in fostering Mohammed Beyd's belief that the jewels were still in his possession, and depend upon the accidents of the future to open an avenue of escape.

Could he contrive to tent with the Arab upon the march north, he might find opportunity in plenty to remove this menace to his life and liberty—it was worth trying, and, further, there seemed no other way out of his difficulty.

"Yes," he said, "Achmet Zek is dead. He fell in battle with a company of Abyssinian cavalry that held me captive. During the fighting I escaped; but I doubt if any of Achmet Zek's men live, and the gold they sought is in the possession of the Abyssinians. Even now they are doubtless marching on this camp, for they were sent by Menelek to punish Achmet Zek and his followers for a raid upon an Abyssinian village. There are many of them, and if we do not make haste to escape we shall all suffer the same fate as Achmet Zek."

Mohammed Beyd listened in silence. How much of the unbeliever's story he might safely believe he did not know; but as it afforded him an excuse for deserting the village and making for the north he was not inclined to cross-question the Belgian too minutely.

"And if I ride north with you," he asked, "half the jewels and half the ransom of the woman shall be mine?"

"Yes," replied Werper.

"Good," said Mohammed Beyd. "I go now to give the order for the breaking of camp early on the morrow," and he rose to leave the tent.

Werper laid a detaining hand upon his arm.

"Wait," he said, "let us determine how many shall accompany us. It is not well that we be burdened by the women and children, for then indeed we might be overtaken by the Abyssinians. It would be far better to select a small guard of your bravest men, and leave word behind that we are riding *west*. Then, when the Abyssinians come they will be put upon the wrong trail should they have it in their hearts to pursue us, and if they do not they will at least ride north with less rapidity than as though they thought that we were ahead of them."

"The serpent is less wise than thou, Werper," said Mohammed Beyd with a smile. "It shall be done as you say. Twenty men shall accompany us, and we shall ride *west*— when we leave the village."

"Good," cried the Belgian, and so it was arranged.

Early the next morning Jane Clayton, after an almost sleepless night, was aroused by the sound of voices outside her prison, and a moment later, M. Frecoult, and two Arabs entered. The latter unbound her ankles and lifted her to her feet. Then her wrists were loosed, she was given a handful of dry bread, and led out into the faint light of dawn.

She looked questioningly at Frecoult, and at a moment that the Arab's attention was attracted in another direction the man leaned toward her and whispered that all was working out as he had planned. Thus assured, the young woman felt a renewal of the hope which the long and miserable night of bondage had almost expunged.

Shortly after, she was lifted to the back of a horse, and surrounded by Arabs, was escorted through the gateway of the village and off into the jungle toward the west. Half an hour later the party turned north, and northerly was their direction for the balance of the march.

M. Frecoult spoke with her but seldom, and she understood that in carrying out his deception he must maintain the semblance of her captor, rather than protector, and so she suspected nothing though she saw the friendly relations which seemed to exist between the European and the Arab leader of the band.

If Werper succeeded in keeping himself from conversation with the young woman, he failed signally to expel her from his thoughts. A hundred times a day he found his eyes wandering in her direction and feasting themselves upon her charms of face and figure. Each hour his infatuation for her grew, until his desire to possess her gained almost the proportions of madness.

If either the girl or Mohammed Beyd could have guessed what passed in the mind of the man which each thought a friend and ally, the apparent harmony of the little company would have been rudely disturbed.

Werper had not succeeded in arranging to tent with Mohammed Beyd, and so he revolved many plans for the assassination of the Arab that would have been greatly simplified had he been permitted to share the other's nightly shelter.

Upon the second day out Mohammed Beyd reined his horse to the side of the animal on which the captive was mounted. It was, apparently, the first notice which the Arab had taken of the girl; but many times during these two days had his cunning eyes peered greedily from beneath the hood of his burnoose to gloat upon the beauties of the prisoner.

Nor was this hidden infatuation of any recent origin. He had conceived it when first the wife of the Englishman had fallen into the hands of Achmet Zek; but while that austere chieftain lived, Mohammed Beyd had not even dared hope for a realization of his imaginings.

Now, though, it was different—only a despised dog of a Christian stood between himself and possession of the girl. How easy it would be to slay the unbeliever, and take unto himself both the woman and the jewels! With the latter in his possession, the ransom which might be obtained for the captive would form no great inducement to her relinquishment in the face of the pleasures of sole ownership of her.

Yes, he would kill Werper, retain all the jewels and keep the Englishwoman.

He turned his eyes upon her as she rode along as his side. How beautiful she was! His fingers opened and closed—skinny, brown talons itching to feel the soft flesh of the victim in their remorseless clutch.

"Do you know," he asked, leaning toward her, "where this man would take you?"

Jane Clayton nodded affirmatively.

"And you are willing to become the plaything of a black sultan?"

The girl drew herself up to her full height, and turned her head away; but she did not reply. She feared lest her knowledge of the ruse that M. Frecoult was playing upon the Arab might cause her to betray herself through an insufficient display of terror and aversion.

"You can escape this fate," continued the Arab; "Mohammed Beyd will save you," and he reached out a brown hand and seized the fingers of her right hand in a grasp so sudden and so fierce that this brutal passion was revealed as clearly in the act as though his lips had confessed it in words.

Jane Clayton wrenched herself from his grasp.

"You beast!" she cried. "Leave me or I shall call M. Frecoult."

Mohammed Beyd drew back with a scowl. His thin, upper lip curled upward, revealing his smooth, white teeth.

"M. Frecoult?" he jeered. "There is no such person. The man's name is Werper. He is a liar, a thief, and a murderer. He killed his captain in the Congo country and fled to the protection of Achmet Zek. He led Achmet Zek to the plunder of your home. He followed your husband, and planned to steal his gold from him. He has told me that you think him your protector, and he has played upon this to win your confidence that it might be easier to carry you north and sell you into some black sultan's harem. Mohammed Beyd is your only hope," and with this assertion to provide the captive with food for thought, the Arab spurred forward toward the head of the column.

Jane Clayton could not know how much of Mohammed Beyd's indictment might be true, or how much false; but at least it had the effect of dampening her hopes and causing her to review with suspicion every past act of the man upon whom she had been looking as her sole protector in the midst of a world of enemies and dangers.

On the march a separate tent had been provided for the

captive, and at night it was pitched between those of Mohammed Beyd and Werper. A sentry was posted at the front and another at the back, and with these precautions it had not been thought necessary to confine the prisoner in bonds.

The evening following her interview with Mohammed Beyd, Jane Clayton sat for some time at the opening of her tent watching the rough activities of the camp. She had eaten the meal that had been brought her by Mohammed Beyd's Negro slave—a meal of cassava cakes and a nondescript stew in which a new-killed monkey, a couple of squirrels and the remains of a zebra, slain the previous day, were impartially and unsavorily combined; but the one-time Baltimore belle had long since submerged in the stern battle for existence, an estheticism which formerly revolted at much slighter provocation.

As the girl's eyes wandered across the trampled jungle clearing, already squalid from the presence of man, she no longer apprehended either the nearer objects of the foreground, the uncouth men laughing or quarreling among themselves, or the jungle beyond, which circumscribed the extreme range of her material vision. Her gaze passed through all these, unseeing, to center itself upon a distant bungalow and scenes of happy security which brought to her eyes tears of mingled joy and sorrow. She saw a tall, broad-shouldered man riding in from distant fields; she saw herself waiting to greet him with an armful of fresh-cut roses from the bushes which flanked the little rustic gate before her. All this was gone, vanished into the past, wiped out by the torches and bullets and hatred of these hideous and degenerate men. With a stifled sob, and a little shudder, Jane Clayton turned back into her tent and sought the pile of unclean blankets which were her bed. Throwing herself face downward upon them she sobbed forth her misery until kindly sleep brought her, at least temporary, relief.

And while she slept a figure stole from the tent that stood to the right of hers. It approached the sentry before the doorway and whispered a few words in the man's ear. The latter nodded, and strode off through the darkness in the direction of his own blankets. The figure passed to the rear of Jane Clayton's tent and spoke again to the sentry there, and this man also left, following in the trail of the first.

Then he who had sent them away stole silently to the tent flap and untying the fastenings entered with the noiselessness of a disembodied spirit.

21

The Flight to the Jungle

SLEEPLESS upon his blankets, Albert Werper let his evil mind dwell upon the charms of the woman in the nearby tent. He had noted Mohammed Beyd's sudden interest in the girl, and judging the man by his own standards, had guessed at the basis of the Arab's sudden change of attitude toward the prisoner.

And as he let his imaginings run riot they aroused within him a bestial jealousy of Mohammed Beyd, and a great fear that the other might encompass his base designs upon the defenseless girl. By a strange process of reasoning, Werper, whose designs were identical with the Arab's, pictured himself as Jane Clayton's protector, and presently convinced himself that the attentions which might seem hideous to her if proffered by Mohammed Beyd, would be welcomed from Albert Werper.

Her husband was dead, and Werper fancied that he could replace in the girl's heart the position which had been vacated by the act of the grim reaper. He could offer Jane Clayton marriage—a thing which Mohammed Beyd would not offer, and which the girl would spurn from him with as deep disgust as she would his unholy lust.

It was not long before the Belgian had succeeded in convincing himself that the captive not only had every reason for having conceived sentiments of love for him; but that she had by various feminine methods acknowledged her new-born affection.

And then a sudden resolution possessed him. He threw the blankets from him and rose to his feet. Pulling on his boots and buckling his cartridge belt and revolver about his hips he stepped to the flap of his tent and looked out. There was no sentry before the entrance to the prisoner's tent! What could it mean? Fate was indeed playing into his hands.

Stepping outside he passed to the rear of the girl's tent. There was no sentry there, either! And now, boldly, he walked to the entrance and stepped within.

Dimly the moonlight illumined the interior. Across the tent a figure bent above the blankets of a bed. There was a whispered word, and another figure rose from the blankets to a sitting position. Slowly Albert Werper's eyes were becoming accustomed to the half darkness of the tent. He saw that the figure leaning over the bed was that of a man, and he guessed at the truth of the nocturnal visitor's identity.

A sullen, jealous rage enveloped him. He took a step in the direction of the two. He heard a frightened cry break from the girl's lips as she recognized the features of the man above her, and he saw Mohammed Beyd seize her by the throat and bear her back upon the blankets.

Cheated passion cast a red blur before the eyes of the Belgian. No! The man should not have her. She was for him and him alone. He would not be robbed of his rights.

Quickly he ran across the tent and threw himself upon the back of Mohammed Beyd. The latter, though surprised by this sudden and unexpected attack, was not one to give up without a battle. The Belgian's fingers were feeling for his throat, but the Arab tore them away, and rising wheeled upon his adversary. As they faced each other Werper struck the Arab a heavy blow in the face, sending him staggering backward. If he had followed up his advantage he would have had Mohammed Beyd at his mercy in another moment; but instead he tugged at his revolver to draw it from its holster, and Fate ordained that at that particular moment the weapon should stick in its leather scabbard.

Before he could disengage it, Mohammed Beyd had recovered himself and was dashing upon him. Again Werper struck the other in the face, and the Arab returned the blow. Striking at each other and ceaselessly attempting to clinch, the two battled about the small interior of the tent, while the girl, wide-eyed in terror and astonishment, watched the duel in frozen silence.

Again and again Werper struggled to draw his weapon. Mohammed Beyd, anticipating no such opposition to his base desires, had come to the tent unarmed, except for a long knife which he now drew as he stood panting during the first brief rest of the encounter.

"Dog of a Christian," he whispered, "look upon this knife in the hands of Mohammed Beyd! Look well, unbeliever, for it is the last thing in life that you shall see or feel. With it Mohammed Beyd will cut out your black heart. If you have a God pray to him now—in a minute more you shall be dead," and with that he rushed viciously upon the Belgian, his knife raised high above his head.

Werper was still dragging futilely at his weapon. The Arab was almost upon him. In desperation the European waited until Mohammed Beyd was all but against him, then he threw himself to one side to the floor of the tent, leaving a leg extended in the path of the Arab.

The trick succeeded. Mohammed Beyd, carried on by

the momentum of his charge, stumbled over the projecting obstacle and crashed to the ground. Instantly he was up again and wheeling to renew the battle; but Werper was on foot ahead of him, and now his revolver, loosened from its holster, flashed in his hand.

The Arab dove headfirst to grapple with him, there was a sharp report, a lurid gleam of flame in the darkness, and Mohammed Beyd rolled over and over upon the floor to come to a final rest beside the bed of the woman he had sought to dishonor.

Almost immediately following the report came the sound of excited voices in the camp without. Men were calling back and forth to one another asking the meaning of the shot. Werper could hear them running hither and thither, investigating.

Jane Clayton had risen to her feet as the Arab died, and now she came forward with outstretched hands toward Werper.

"How can I ever thank you, my friend?" she asked. "And to think that only today I had almost believed the infamous story which this beast told me of your perfidy and of your past. Forgive me, M. Frecoult. I might have known that a white man and a gentleman could be naught else than the protector of a woman of his own race amid the dangers of this savage land."

Werper's hands dropped limply at his sides. He stood looking at the girl; but he could find no words to reply to her. Her innocent arraignment of his true purposes was unanswerable.

Outside, the Arabs were searching for the author of the disturbing shot. The two sentries who had been relieved and sent to their blankets by Mohammed Beyd were the first to suggest going to the tent of the prisoner. It occurred to them that possibly the woman had successfully defended herself against their leader.

Werper heard the men approaching. To be apprehended as the slayer of Mohammed Beyd would be equivalent to a sentence of immediate death. The fierce and brutal raiders would tear to pieces a Christian who had dared spill the blood of their leader. He must find some excuse to delay the finding of Mohammed Beyd's dead body.

Returning his revolver to its holster, he walked quickly to the entrance of the tent. Parting the flaps he stepped out and confronted the men, who were rapidly approaching. Somehow he found within him the necessary bravado to force a smile to his lips, as he held up his hand to bar their farther progress.

"The woman resisted," he said, "and Mohammed Beyd was forced to shoot her. She is not dead—only slightly wounded. You may go back to your blankets. Mohammed Beyd and I will look after the prisoner;" then he turned and re-entered the tent, and the raiders, satisfied by this explanation, gladly returned to their broken slumbers.

As he again faced Jane Clayton, Werper found himself animated by quite different intentions than those which had lured him from his blankets but a few minutes before. The excitement of his encounter with Mohammed Beyd, as well as the dangers which he now faced at the hands of the raiders when morning must inevitably reveal the truth of what had occurred in the tent of the prisoner that night, had naturally cooled the hot passion which had dominated him when he entered the tent.

But another and stronger force was exerting itself in the girl's favor. However low a man may sink, honor and chivalry, has he ever possessed them, are never entirely eradicated from his character, and though Albert Werper had long since ceased to evidence the slightest claim to either the one or the other, the spontaneous acknowledgment of them which the girl's speech had presumed had reawakened them both within him.

For the first time he realized the almost hopeless and frightful position of the fair captive, and the depths of ignominy to which he had sunk, that had made it possible for him, a well-born, European gentleman, to have entertained even for a moment the part that he had taken in the ruin of her home, happiness, and herself.

Too much of baseness already lay at the threshold of his conscience for him ever to hope entirely to redeem himself; but in the first, sudden burst of contrition the man conceived an honest intention to undo, in so far as lay within his power, the evil that his criminal avaice had brought upon this sweet and unoffending woman.

As he stood apparently listening to the retreating foot-his power, the evil that his criminal avarice had brought Jane Clayton approached him.

"What are we to do now?" she asked. "Morning will bring discovery of this," and she pointed to the still body of Mohammed Beyd. "They will kill you when they find him."

For a time Werper did not reply, then he turned suddenly toward the woman.

"I have a plan," he cried. "It will require nerve and courage on your part; but you have already shown that you possess both. Can you endure still more?"

"I can endure anything," she replied with a brave smile,

"that may offer us even a slight chance for escape."

"You must simulate death," he explained, "while I carry you from the camp. I will explain to the sentries that Mohammed Beyd has ordered me to take your body into the jungle. This seemingly unnecessary act I shall explain upon the grounds that Mohammed Beyd had conceived a violent passion for you and that he so regretted the act by which he had become your slayer that he could not endure the silent reproach of your lifeless body."

The girl held up her hand to stop. A smile touched her lips.

"Are you quite mad?" she asked. "Do you imagine that the sentries will credit any such ridiculous tale?"

"You do not know them," he replied. "Beneath their rough exteriors, despite their calloused and criminal natures, there exists in each a well-defined strain of romantic emotionalism —you will find it among such as these throughout the world. It is romance which lures men to lead wild lives of outlawry and crime. The ruse will succeed—never fear."

Jane Clayton shrugged. "We can but try it—and then what?"

"I shall hide you in the jungle," continued the Belgian, "coming for you alone and with two horses in the morning."

"But how will you explain Mohammed Beyd's death?" she asked. "It will be discovered before ever you can escape the camp in the morning."

"I shall not explain it," replied Werper. "Mohammed Beyd shall explain it himself—we must leave that to him. Are you ready for the venture?"

"Yes."

"But wait, I must get you a weapon and ammunition," and Werper walked quickly from the tent.

Very shortly he returned with an extra revolver and ammunition belt strapped about his waist.

"Are you ready?" he asked.

"Quite ready," replied the girl.

"Then come and throw yourself limply across my left shoulder," and Werper knelt to receive her.

"There," he said, as he rose to his feet. "Now, let your arms, your legs and your head hang limply. Remember that you are dead."

A moment later the man walked out into the camp, the body of the woman across his shoulder.

A thorn boma had been thrown up about the camp, to discourage the bolder of the hungry carnivora. A couple of sentries paced to and fro in the light of a fire which they kept

burning brightly. The nearer of these looked up in surprise as
he saw Werper approaching.

"Who are you?" he cried. "What have you there?"

Werper raised the hood of his burnoose that the fellow
might see his face.

"This is the body of the woman," he explained. "Mohammed Beyd has asked me to take it into the jungle, for he cannot bear to look upon the face of her whom he loved, and
whom necessity compelled him to slay. He suffers greatly—he
is inconsolable. It was with difficulty that I prevented him taking his own life."

Across the speaker's shoulder, limp and frightened, the girl
waited for the Arab's reply. He would laugh at this preposterous story; of that she was sure. In an instant he would un-
mask the deception that M. Frecoult was attempting to prac-
tice upon him, and they would both be lost. She tried to plan
how best she might aid her would-be rescuer in the fight
which must most certainly follow within a moment or two.

Then she heard the voice of the Arab as he replied to M.
Frecoult.

"Are you going alone, or do you wish me to awaken someone to accompany you?" he asked, and his tone denoted not
the least surprise that Mohammed Beyd had suddenly discovered such remarkably sensitive characteristics.

"I shall go alone," replied Werper, and he passed on and
out through the narrow opening in the boma, by which the
sentry stood.

A moment later he had entered among the boles of the
trees with his burden, and when safely hidden from the sentry's view lowered the girl to her feet, with a low, "sh-sh,"
when she would have spoken.

Then he led her a little farther into the forest, halted beneath a large tree with spreading branches, buckled a cartridge belt and revolver about her waist, and assisted her to
clamber into the lower branches.

"Tomorrow," he whispered, "as soon as I can elude them,
I will return for you. Be brave, Lady Greystoke—we may
yet escape."

"Thank you," she replied in a low tone. "You have been
very kind, and very brave."

Werper did not reply, and the darkness of the night hid
the scarlet flush of shame which swept upward across his
face. Quickly he turned and made his way back to camp.
The sentry, from his post, saw him enter his own tent;
but he did not see him crawl under the canvas at the rear
and sneak cautiously to the tent which the prisoner had occupied, where now lay the dead body of Mohammed Beyd.

Raising the lower edge of the rear wall, Werper crept within and approached the corpse. Without an instant's hesitation he seized the dead wrists and dragged the body upon its back to the point where he had just entered. On hands and knees he backed out as he had come in, drawing the corpse after him. Once outside the Belgian crept to the side of the tent and surveyed as much of the camp as lay within his vision —no one was watching.

Returning to the body, he lifted it to his shoulder, and risking all on a quick sally, ran swiftly across the narrow opening which separated the prisoner's tent from that of the dead man. Behind the silken wall he halted and lowered his burden to the ground, and there he remained motionless for several minutes, listening.

Satisfied, at last, that no one had seen him, he stooped and raised the bottom of the tent wall, backed in and dragged the thing that had been Mohammed Beyd after him. To the sleeping rugs of the dead raider he drew the corpse, then he fumbled about in the darkness until he had found Mohammed Beyd's revolver. With the weapon in his hand he returned to the side of the dead man, kneeled beside the bedding, and inserted his right hand with the weapon beneath the rugs, piled a number of thicknesses of the closely woven fabric over and about the revolver with his left hand. Then he pulled the trigger, and at the same instant he coughed.

The muffled report could not have been heard above the sound of his cough by one directly outside the tent. Werper was satisfied. A grim smile touched his lips as he withdrew the weapon from the rugs and placed it carefully in the right hand of the dead man, fixing three of the fingers around the grip and the index finger inside the trigger guard.

A moment longer he tarried to rearrange the disordered rugs, and then he left as he had entered, fastening down the rear wall of the tent as it had been before he had raised it.

Going to the tent of the prisoner he removed there also the evidence that someone might have come or gone beneath the rear wall. Then he returned to his own tent, entered, fastened down the canvas, and crawled into his blankets.

The following morning he was awakened by the excited voice of Mohammed Beyd's slave calling to him at the entrance of his tent.

"Quick! Quick!" cried the black in a frightened tone. "Come! Mohammed Beyd is dead in his tent—dead by his own hand."

Werper sat up quickly in his blankets at the first alarm, a startled expression upon his countenance; but at the last words of the black a sigh of relief escaped his lips and a slight smile replaced the tense lines upon his face.

"I come," he called to the slave, and drawing on his boots, rose and went out of his tent.

Excited Arabs and blacks were running from all parts of the camp toward the silken tent of Mohammed Beyd, and when Werper entered he found a number of the raiders crowded about the corpse, now cold and stiff.

Shouldering his way among them, the Belgian halted beside the dead body of the raider. He looked down in silence for a moment upon the still face, then he wheeled upon the Arabs.

"Who has done this thing?" he cried. His tone was both menacing and accusing. "Who has murdered Mohammed Beyd?"

A sudden chorus of voices arose in tumultuous protest.

"Mohammed Beyd was not murdered," they cried. "He died by his own hand. This, and Allah, are our witnesses," and they pointed to a revolver in the dead man's hand.

For a time Werper pretended to be skeptical; but at last permitted himself to be convinced that Mohammed Beyd had indeed killed himself in remorse for the death of the white woman he had, all unknown to his followers, loved so devotedly.

Werper himself wrapped the blankets of the dead man about the corpse, taking care to fold inward the scorched and bullet-torn fabric that had muffled the report of the weapon he had fired the night before. Then six husky blacks carried the body out into the clearing where the camp stood, and deposited it in a shallow grave. As the loose earth fell upon the silent form beneath the tell-tale blankets, Albert Werper heaved another sigh of relief—his plan had worked out even better than he had dared hope.

With Achmet Zek and Mohammed Beyd both dead, the raiders were without a leader, and after a brief conference they decided to return into the north on visits to the various tribes to which they belonged. Werper, after learning the direction they intended taking, announced that for his part, he was going east to the coast, and as they knew of nothing he possessed which any of them coveted, they signified their willingness that he should go his way.

As they rode off, he sat his horse in the center of the clearing watching them disappear one by one into the jungle, and thanked his God that he had at last escaped their villainous clutches.

When he could no longer hear any sound of them, he turned to the right and rode into the forest toward the tree where he had hidden Lady Greystoke, and drawing rein beneath it, called up in a gay and hopeful voice a pleasant, "Good morning!"

There was no reply, and though his eyes searched the thick foliage above him, he could see no sign of the girl. Dismounting, he quickly climbed into the tree, where he could obtain a view of all its branches. The tree was empty —Jane Clayton had vanished during the silent watches of the jungle night.

22

Tarzan Recovers His Reason

As TARZAN let the pebbles from the recovered pouch run through his fingers, his thoughts returned to the pile of yellow ingots about which the Arabs and the Abyssinians had waged their relentless battle.

What was there in common between that pile of dirty metal and the beautiful, sparkling pebbles that had formerly been in his pouch? What was the metal? From whence had it come? What was that tantalizing half-conviction which seemed to demand the recognition of his memory that the yellow pile for which these men had fought and died had been intimately connected with his past—that it had been his?

What had been his past? He shook his head. Vaguely the memory of his apish childhood passed slowly in review—then came a strangely tangled mass of faces, figures and events which seemed to have no relation to Tarzan of the Apes, and yet which were, even in their fragmentary form, familiar.

Slowly and painfully, recollection was attempting to reassert itself, the hurt brain was mending, as the cause of its recent failure to function was being slowly absorbed or removed by the healing processes of perfect circulation.

The people who now passed before his mind's eye for the first time in weeks wore familiar faces; but yet he could neither place them in the niches they had once filled in his past life, nor call them by name. One was a fair she, and it was her face which most often moved through the tangled recollections of his convalescing brain. Who was she? What she been to Tarzan of the Apes? He seemed to see her about the very spot upon which the pile of gold had been unearthed by the Abyssinians; but the surroundings were vastly different from those which now obtained.

There was a building—there were many buildings—and there were hedges, fences, and flowers. Tarzan puckered his brow in puzzled study of the wonderful problem. For an instant he seemed to grasp the whole of a true explanation, and then, just as success was within his grasp, the picture faded into a jungle scene where a naked, white youth danced in company with a band of hairy, primordial ape-things.

Tarzan shook his head and sighed. Why was it that he could not recollect? At least he was sure that in some way the pile of gold, the place where it lay, the subtle aroma of the elusive she he had been pursuing, the memory figure of the white woman, and he himself, were inextricably connected by the ties of a forgotten past.

If the woman belonged there, what better place to search or await her than the very spot which his broken recollections seemed to assign to her? It was worth trying. Tarzan slipped the thong of the empty pouch over his shoulder and started off through the trees in the direction of the plain.

At the outskirts of the forest he met the Arabs returning in search of Achmet Zek. Hiding, he let them pass, and then resumed his way toward the charred ruins of the home he had been almost upon the point of recalling to his memory.

His journey across the plain was interrupted by the discovery of a small herd of antelope in a little swale, where the cover and the wind were well combined to make stalking easy. A fat yearling rewarded a half hour of stealthy creeping and a sudden, savage rush, and it was late in the afternoon when the ape-man settled himself upon his haunches beside his kill to enjoy the fruits of his skill, his cunning, and his prowess.

His hunger satisfied, thirst next claimed his attention. The river lured him by the shortest path toward its refreshing waters, and when he had drunk, night already had fallen and he was some half mile or more down stream from the point where he had seen the pile of yellow ingots, and where he hoped to meet the memory woman, or find some clew to her whereabouts or her identity.

To the jungle bred, time is usually a matter of small moment, and haste, except when engendered by terror, by rage, or by hunger, is distasteful. Today was gone. Therefore tomorrow, of which there was an infinite procession, would answer admirably for Tarzan's further quest. And, besides, the ape-man was tired and would sleep.

A tree afforded him the safety, seclusion and comforts of a

well-appointed bedchamber, and to the chorus of the hunters
and the hunted of the wild river bank he soon dropped off
into deep slumber.

Morning found him both hungry and thirsty again, and
dropping from his tree he made his way to the drinking
place at the river's edge. There he found Numa, the lion,
ahead of him. The big fellow was lapping the water greedily,
and at the approach of Tarzan along the trail in his rear, he
raised his head, and turning his gaze backward across his
maned shoulders glared at the intruder. A low growl of
warning rumbled from his throat; but Tarzan, guessing that
the beast had but just quitted his kill and was well filled,
merely made a slight detour and continued to the river,
where he stopped a few yards above the tawny cat, and dropping upon his hands and knees plunged his face into the cool
water. For a moment the lion continued to eye the man; then
he resumed his drinking, and man and beast quenched their
thirst side by side each apparently oblivious of the other's
presence.

Numa was the first to finish. Raising his head, he gazed
across the river for a few minutes with that stony fixity of
attention which is a characteristic of his kind. But for the
ruffling of his black mane to the touch of the passing breeze
he might have been wrought from golden bronze, so motionless, so statuesque his pose.

A deep sigh from the cavernous lungs dispelled the illusion.
The mighty head swung slowly around until the yellow eyes
rested upon the man. The bristled lip curved upward, expos-
ing yellow fangs. Another warning growl vibrated the heavy
jowls, and the king of beasts turned majestically about and
paced slowly up the trail into the dense reeds.

Tarzan of the Apes drank on, but from the corners of his
gray eyes he watched the great brute's every move until
he had disappeared from view, and, after, his keen ears
marked the movements of the carnivore.

A plunge in the river was followed by a scant breakfast of
eggs which chance discovered to him, and then he set off
up river toward the ruins of the bungalow where the golden
ingots had marked the center of yesterday's battle.

And when he came upon the spot, great was his surprise
and consternation, for the yellow metal had disappeared.
The earth, trampled by the feet of horses and men, gave no
clew. It was as though the ingots had evaporated into thin air.

The ape-man was at a loss to know where to turn or what
next to do. There was no sign of any spoor which might
denote that the she had been here. The metal was gone, and
if there was any connection between the she and the metal

it seemed useless to wait for her now that the latter had been removed elsewhere.

Everything seemed to elude him—the pretty pebbles, the yellow metal, the she, his memory. Tarzan was disgusted. He would go back into the jungle and look for Chulk, and so he turned his steps once more toward the forest. He moved rapidly, swinging across the plain in a long, easy trot, and at the edge of the forest, taking to the trees with the agility and speed of a small monkey.

His direction was aimless—he merely raced on and on through the jungle, the joy of unfettered action his principal urge, with the hope of stumbling upon some clew to Chulk or the she, a secondary incentive.

For two days he roamed about, killing, eating, drinking and sleeping wherever inclination and the means to indulge it occurred simultaneously. It was upon the morning of the third day that the scent spoor of horse and man were wafted faintly to his nostrils. Instantly he altered his course to glide silently through the branches in the direction from which the scent came.

It was not long before he came upon a solitary horseman riding toward the east. Instantly his eyes confirmed what his nose had previously suspected—the rider was he who had stolen his pretty pebbles. The light of rage flared suddenly in the gray eyes as the ape-man dropped lower among the branches until he moved almost directly above the unconscious Werper.

There was a quick leap, and the Belgian felt a heavy body hurtle onto the rump of his terror-stricken mount. The horse, snorting, leaped forward. Giant arms encircled the rider, and in the twinkling of an eye he was dragged from his saddle to find himself lying in the narrow trail with a naked, white giant kneeling upon his breast.

Recognition came to Werper with the first glance at his captor's face, and a pallor of fear overspread his features. Strong fingers were at his throat, fingers of steel. He tried to cry out, to plead for his life; but the cruel fingers denied him speech, as they were as surely denying him life.

"The pretty pebbles?" cried the man upon his breast. "What did you with the pretty pebbles—with Tarzan's pretty pebbles?"

The fingers relaxed to permit of a reply. For some time Werper could only choke and cough—at last he regained the powers of speech.

"Achmet Zek, the Arab, stole them from me," he cried; "he made me give up the pouch and the pebbles."

"I saw all that," replied Tarzan; "but the pebbles in the

pouch were not the pebbles of Tarzan—they were only such pebbles as fill the bottoms of the rivers, and the shelving banks beside them. Even the Arab would not have them, for he threw them away in anger when he had looked upon them. It is my pretty pebbles that I want—where are they?"

"I do not know, I do not know," cried Werper. "I gave them to Achmet Zek or he would have killed me. A few minutes later he followed me along the trail to slay me, although he had promised to molest me no further, and I shot and killed him; but the pouch was not upon his person and though I searched about the jungle for some time I could not find it."

"I found it, I tell you," growled Tarzan, "and I also found the pebbles which Achmet Zek had thrown away in disgust. They were not Tarzan's pebbles. You have hidden them! Tell me where they are or I will kill you," and the brown fingers of the ape-man closed a little tighter upon the throat of his victim.

Werper struggled to free himself. "My God, Lord Greystoke," he managed to scream, "would you commit murder for a handful of stones?"

The fingers at his throat relaxed, a puzzled, far-away expression softened the gray eyes.

"Lord Greystoke!" repeated the ape-man. "Lord Greystoke! Who is Lord Greystoke? Where have I heard that name before?"

"Why man, you are Lord Greystoke," cried the Belgian. "You were injured by a falling rock when the earthquake shattered the passage to the underground chamber to which you and your black Waziri had come to fetch golden ingots back to your bungalow. The blow shattered your memory. You are John Clayton, Lord Greystoke—don't you remember?"

"John Clayton, Lord Greystoke!" repeated Tarzan. Then for a moment he was silent. Presently his hand went falteringly to his forehead, an expression of wonderment filled his eyes—of wonderment and sudden understanding. The forgotten name had reawakened the returning memory that had been struggling to reassert itself. The ape-man relinquished his grasp upon the throat of the Belgian, and leaped to his feet.

"God!" he cried, and then, "Jane!" Suddenly he turned toward Werper. "My wife?" he asked. "What has become of her? The farm is in ruins. You know. You have had something to do with all this. You followed me to Opar, you stole the jewels which I thought but pretty pebbles. You are a crook! Do not try to tell me that you are not."

"He is worse than a crook," said a quiet voice close behind them.

Tarzan turned in astonishment to see a tall man in uniform standing in the trail a few paces from him. Back of the man were a number of black soldiers in the uniform of the Congo Free State.

"He is a murderer, Monsieur," continued the officer. "I have followed him for a long time to take him back to stand trial for the killing of his superior officer."

Werper was upon his feet now, gazing, white and trembling, at the fate which had overtaken him even in the fastness of the labyrinthine jungle. Instinctively he turned to flee; but Tarzan of the Apes reached out a strong hand and grasped him by the shoulder.

"Wait!" said the ape-man to his captive. "This gentleman wishes you, and so do I. When I am through with you, he may have you. Tell me what has become of my wife."

The Belgian officer eyed the almost naked, white giant with curiosity. He noted the strange contrast of primitive weapons and apparel, and the easy, fluent French which the man spoke. The former denoted the lowest, the latter the highest type of culture. He could not quite determine the social status of this strange creature; but he knew that he did not relish the easy assurance with which the fellow presumed to dictate when he might take possession of the prisoner.

"Pardon me," he said, stepping forward and placing his hand on Werper's other shoulder; "but this gentleman is my prisoner. He must come with me."

"When I am through with him," replied Tarzan, quietly.

The officer turned and beckoned to the soldiers standing in the trail behind him. A company of uniformed blacks stepped quickly forward and pushing past the three, surrounded the ape-man and his captive.

"Both the law and the power to enforce it are upon my side," announced the officer. "Let us have no trouble. If you have a grievance against this man you may return with me and enter your charge regularly before an authorized tribunal."

"Your legal rights are not above suspicion, my friend," replied Tarzan, "and your power to enforce your comands are only apparent—not real. You have presumed to enter British territory with an armed force. Where is your authority for this invasion? Where are the extradition papers which warrant the arrest of this man? And what assurance have you that I cannot bring an armed force about you that will prevent your return to the Congo Free State?"

The Belgian lost his temper. "I have no disposition to

argue with a naked savage," he cried. "Unless you wish to be hurt you will not interfere with me. Take the prisoner, Sergeant!"

Werper raised his lips close to Tarzan's ear. "Keep me from them, and I can show you the very spot where I saw your wife last night," he whispered. "She cannot be far from here at this very minute."

The soldiers, following the signal from their sergeant, closed in to seize Werper. Tarzan grabbed the Belgian about the waist, and bearing him beneath his arm as he might have borne a sack of flour, leaped forward in an attempt to break through the cordon. His right fist caught the nearest soldier upon the jaw and sent him hurtling backward upon his fellows. Clubbed rifles were torn from the hands of those who barred his way, and right and left the black soldiers stumbled aside in the face of the ape-man's savage break for liberty.

So completely did the blacks surround the two that they dared not fire for fear of hitting one of their own number, and Tarzan was already through them and upon the point of dodging into the concealing mazes of the jungle when one who had sneaked upon him from behind struck him a heavy blow upon the head with a rifle.

In an instant the ape-man was down and a dozen black soldiers were upon his back. When he regained consciousness he found himself securely bound, as was Werper also. The Belgian officer, success having crowned his efforts, was in good humor, and inclined to chaff his prisoners about the ease with which they had been captured; but from Tarzan of the Apes he elicited no response. Werper, however, was voluble in his protests. He explained that Tarzan was an English lord; but the officer only laughed at the assertion, and advised his prisoner to save his breath for his defense in court.

As soon as Tarzan regained his senses and it was found that he was not seriously injured, the prisoners were hastened into line and the return march toward the Congo Free State boundary commenced.

Toward evening the column halted beside a stream, made camp and prepared the evening meal. From the thick foliage of the nearby jungle a pair of fierce eyes watched the activities of the uniformed blacks with silent intensity and curiosity. From beneath beetling brows the creature saw the boma constructed, the fires built, and the supper prepared.

Tarzan and Werper had been lying bound behind a small pile of knapsacks from the time that the company had halted; but with the preparation of the meal completed, their guard ordered them to rise and come forward to one of the fires where their hands would be unfettered that they might eat.

As the giant ape-man rose, a startled expression of recognition entered the eyes of the watcher in the jungle, and a low guttural broke from the savage lips. Instantly Tarzan was alert, but the answering growl died upon his lips, suppressed by the fear that it might arouse the suspicions of the soldiers.

Suddenly an inspiration came to him. He turned toward Werper.

"I am going to speak to you in a loud voice and in a tongue which you do not understand. Appear to listen intently to what I say, and occasionally mumble something as though replying in the same language—our escape may hinge upon the success of your efforts."

Werper nodded in assent and understanding, and immediately there broke from the lips of his companion a strange jargon which might have been compared with equal propriety to the barking and growling of a dog and the chattering of monkeys.

The nearer soldiers looked in surprise at the ape-man. Some of them laughed, while others drew away in evident superstitious fear. The officer approached the prisoners while Tarzan was still jabbering, and halted behind them, listening in perplexed interest. When Werper mumbled some ridiculous jargon in reply his curiosity broke bounds, and he stepped forward, demanding to know what language it was that they spoke.

Tarzan had gauged the measure of the man's culture from the nature and quality of his conversation during the march, and he rested the success of his reply upon the estimate he had made.

"Greek," he explained.

"Oh, I thought it was Greek," replied the officer; "but it has been so many years since I studied it that I was not sure. In future, however, I will thank you to speak in a language which I am more familiar with."

Werper turned his head to hide a grin, whispering to Tarzan: "It was Greek to him all right—and to me, too."

But one of the black soldiers mumbled in a low voice to a companion: "I have heard those sounds before—once at night when I was lost in the jungle, I heard the hairy men of the trees talking among themselves, and their words were like the words of this white man. I wish that we had not found him. He is not a man at all—he is a bad spirit, and we shall have bad luck if we do not let him go," and the fellow rolled his eyes fearfully toward the jungle.

His companion laughed nervously, and moved away, to

repeat the conversation, with variations and exaggerations, to others of the black soldiery, so that it was not long before a frightful tale of black magic and sudden death was woven about the giant prisoner, and had gone the rounds of the camp.

And deep in the gloomy jungle amidst the darkening shadows of the falling night a hairy, manlike creature swung swiftly southward upon some secret mission of his own.

23

A Night of Terror

TO JANE CLAYTON, waiting in the tree where Werper had placed her, it seemed that the long night would never end, yet end it did at last, and within an hour of the coming of dawn her spirits leaped with renewed hope at sight of a solitary horseman approaching along the trail.

The flowing burnoose, with its loose hood, hid both the face and the figure of the rider; but that it was M. Frecoult the girl well knew, since he had been garbed as an Arab, and he alone might be expected to seek her hiding place.

That which she saw relieved the strain of the long night vigil; but there was much that she did not see. She did not see the black face beneath the white hood, nor the file of ebon horsemen beyond the trail's bend riding slowly in the wake of their leader. These things she did not see at first, and so she leaned downward toward the approaching rider, a cry of welcome forming in her throat.

At the first word the man looked up, reining in in surprise, and as she saw the black face of Abdul Mourak, the Abyssinian, she shrank back in terror among the branches; but it was too late. The man had seen her, and now he called to her to descend. At first she refused; but when a dozen black cavalrymen drew up behind their leader, and at Abdul Mourak's command one of them started to climb the tree after her she realized that resistance was futile, and came slowly down to stand upon the ground before this new captor and plead her cause in the name of justice and humanity.

Angered by recent defeat, and by the loss of the gold, the jewels, and his prisoners, Abdul Mourak was in no mood to be influenced by any appeal to those softer sentiments to which, as a matter of fact, he was almost a stranger even under the most favourable conditions.

He looked for degredation and possible death in punishment for his failures and his misfortunes when he should have returned to his native land and made his report to Menelek; but an acceptable gift might temper the wrath of the emperor, and surely this fair flower of another race should be gratefully received by the black ruler!

When Jane Clayton had concluded her appeal, Abdul Mourak replied briefly that he would promise her protection; but that he must take her to his emperor. The girl did not need ask him why, and once again hope died within her breast. Resignedly she permitted herself to be lifted to a seat behind one of the troopers, and again, under new masters, her journey was resumed toward what she now began to believe was her inevitable fate.

Abdul Mourak, bereft of his guides by the battle he had waged against the raiders, and himself unfamiliar with the country, had wandered far from the trail he should have followed, and as a result had made but little progress toward the north since the beginning of his flight. Today he was beating toward the west in the hope of coming upon a village where he might obtain guides; but night found him still as far from a realization of his hopes as had the rising sun.

It was a dispirited company which went into camp, waterless and hungry, in the dense jungle. Attracted by the horses, lions roared about the boma, and to their hideous din was added the shrill neighs of the terror-stricken beasts they hunted. There was little sleep for man or beast, and the sentries were doubled that there might be enough on duty both to guard against the sudden charge of an overbold, or overhungry lion, and to keep the fire blazing which was an even more effectual barrier against them than the thorny boma.

It was well past midnight, and as yet Jane Clayton, notwithstanding that she had passed a sleepless night the night before, had scarcely more than dozed. A sense of impending danger seemed to hang like a black pall over the camp. The veteran troopers of the black emperor were nervous and ill at ease. Abdul Mourak left his blankets a dozen times to pace restlessly back and forth between the tethered horses and the crackling fire. The girl could see his great frame silhouetted against the lurid glare of the flames, and she guessed from the quick, nervous movements of the man that he was afraid.

The roaring of the lions rose in sudden fury until the earth trembled to the hideous chorus. The horses shrilled their neighs of terror as they lay back upon their halter ropes in their mad endeavors to break loose. A trooper, braver than his fellows, leaped among the kicking, plunging, fear-maddened beasts in a futile attempt to quiet them. A lion, large, and fierce, and courageous, leaped almost to the boma, full in the bright light from the fire. A sentry raised his piece and fired, and the little leaden pellet unstoppered the vials of hell upon the terror-stricken camp.

The shot ploughed a deep and painful furrow in the lion's side, arousing all the bestial fury of the little brain; but abating not a whit the power and vigor of the great body.

Unwounded, the boma and the flames might have turned him back; but now the pain and the rage wiped caution from his mind, and with a loud, and angry roar he topped the barrier with an easy leap and was among the horses.

What had been pandemonium before became now an indescribable tumult of hideous sound. The stricken horse upon which the lion leaped shrieked out its terror and its agony. Several about it broke their tethers and plunged madly about the camp. Men leaped from their blankets and with guns ready ran toward the picket line, and then from the jungle beyond the boma a dozen lions, emboldened by the example of their fellow charged fearlessly upon the camp.

Singly and in twos and threes they leaped the boma, until the little enclosure was filled with cursing men and screaming horses battling for their lives with the green-eyed devils of the jungle.

With the charge of the first lion, Jane Clayton had scramble to her feet, and now she stood horror-struck at the scene of savage slaughter that swirled and eddied about her. Once a bolting horse knocked her down, and a moment later a lion, leaping in pursuit of another terror-stricken animal, brushed her so closely that she was again thrown from her feet.

Amidst the cracking of the rifles and the growls of the carnivora rose the death screams of stricken men and horses as they were dragged down by the blood-mad cats. The leaping carnivora and the plunging horses, prevented any concerted action by the Abyssinians—it was every man for himself—and in the melee, the defenseless woman was either forgotten or ignored by her black captors. A score of times was her life menaced by charging lions, by plunging horses, or by the wildly fired bullets of the frightened troopers, yet there was no chance of escape, for now with the fiendish cunning of their kind, the tawny hunters commenced to circle about their prey, hemming them within a ring of mighty, yellow fangs, and sharp, long talons. Again and again an individual lion would dash suddenly among the frightened men and horses, and occasionally a horse, goaded to frenzy by pain or terror, succeeded in racing safely through the circling lions, leaping the boma, and escaping into the jungle; but for the men and the woman no such escape was possible.

A horse, struck by a stray bullet, fell beside Jane Clayton, a lion leaped across the expiring beast full upon the breast of a black trooper just beyond. The man clubbed his rifle and struck futilely at the broad head, and then he was down and the carnivore was standing above him.

Shrieking out his terror, the soldier clawed with puny fingers at the shaggy breast in vain endeavor to push away the grinning jaws. The lion lowered his head, the gaping fangs closed with a single sickening crunch upon the fear-distorted face, and turning strode back across the body of the dead horse dragging his limp and bloody burden with him.

Wide-eyed the girl stood watching. She saw the carnivore step upon the corpse, stumblingly, as the grisly thing swung between its forepaws, and her eyes remained fixed in fascination while the beast passed within a few paces of her.

The interference of the body seemed to enrage the lion. He shook the inanimate clay venomously. He growled and roared hideously at the dead, insensate thing, and then he dropped it and raised his head to look about in search of some living victim upon which to wreak his ill temper. His yellow eyes fastened themselves balefully upon the figure of the girl, the bristling lips raised, disclosing the grinning fangs. A terrific roar broke from the savage throat, and the great beast crouched to spring upon this new and helpless victim.

Quiet had fallen early upon the camp where Tarzan and Werper lay securely bound. Two nervous sentries paced their beats, their eyes rolling often toward the impenetrable shadows of the gloomy jungle. The others slept or tried to sleep —all but the ape-man. Silently and powerfully he strained at the bonds which fettered his wrists.

The muscles knotted beneath the smooth, brown skin of his arms and shoulders, the veins stood out upon his temples from the force of his exertions—a strand parted, another and another, and one hand was free. Then from the jungle came a low guttural, and the ape-man became suddenly a silent, rigid statue, with ears and nostrils straining to span the black void where his eyesight could not reach.

Again came the uncanny sound from the thick verdure beyond the camp. A sentry halted abruptly, straining his eyes into the gloom. The kinky wool upon his head stiffened and raised. He called to his comrade in a hoarse whisper.

"Did you hear it?" he asked.

The other came closer, trembling.

"Hear what?"

Again was the weird sound repeated, followed almost immediately by a similar and answering sound from the camp. The sentries drew close together, watching the black spot from which the voice seemed to come.

Trees overhung the boma at this point which was upon the opposite side of the camp from them. They dared not approach. Their terror even prevented them from arousing their fellows—they could only stand in frozen fear and watch for the fearsome apparition they momentarily expected to see leap from the jungle.

Nor had they long to wait. A dim, bulky form dropped lightly from the branches of a tree into the camp. At sight of it one of the sentries recovered command of his muscles and his voice. Screaming loudly to awaken the sleeping camp, he leaped toward the flickering watch fire and threw a mass of brush upon it.

The white officer and the black soldiers sprang from their blankets. The flames leaped high upon the rejuvenated fire, lighting the entire camp, and the awakened men shrank back in superstitious terror from the sight that met their frightened and astonished vision.

A dozen huge and hairy forms loomed large beneath the trees at the far side of the enclosure. The white giant, one hand freed, had struggled to his knees and was calling to the frightful, nocturnal visitors in a hideous medley of bestial gutturals, barkings and growlings.

Werper had managed to sit up. He, too, saw the savage faces of the approaching anthropoids and scarcely knew whether to be relieved or terror-stricken.

Growling, the great apes leaped forward toward Tarzan and Werper. Chulk led them. The Belgian officer called to his men to fire upon the intruders; but the Negroes held back, filled as they were with superstitious terror of the hairy treemen, and with the conviction that the white giant who could thus summon the beasts of the jungle to his aid was more than human.

Drawing his own weapon, the officer fired, and Tarzan fearing the effect of the noise upon his really timid friends called to them to hasten and fulfill his commands.

A couple of the apes turned and fled at the sound of the firearm; but Chulk and a half dozen others waddled rapidly forward, and, following the ape-man's directions, seized both him and Werper and bore them off toward the jungle.

By dint of threats, reproaches and profanity the Belgian officer succeeded in persuading his trembling command to fire a volley after the retreating apes. A ragged, straggling volley it was, but at least one of its bullets found a mark, for as the jungle closed about the hairy rescuers, Chulk, who bore Werper across one broad shoulder, staggered and fell.

In an instant he was up again; but the Belgian guessed from his unsteady gait that he was hard hit. He lagged far behind the others, and it was several minutes after they had halted at Tarzan's command before he came slowly up to them, reeling from side to side, and at last falling again beneath the weight of his burden and the shock of his wound.

As Chulk went down he dropped Werper, so that the latter fell face downward with the body of the ape lying half across him. In this position the Belgian felt something resting against his hands, which were still bound at his back—something that was not a part of the hairy body of the ape.

Mechanically the man's fingers felt of the object resting almost in their grasp—it was a soft pouch, filled with small, hard particles. Werper gasped in wonderment as recognition filtered through the incredulity of his mind. It was impossible, and yet—it was true!

Feverishly he strove to remove the pouch from the ape and transfer it to his own possession; but the restricted radius to which his bonds held his hands prevented this, though he did succeed in tucking the pouch with its precious contents inside the waist band of his trousers.

Tarzan, sitting at a short distance, was busy with the remaining knots of the cords which bound him. Presently he flung aside the last of them and rose to his feet. Approaching Werper he knelt beside him. For a moment he examined the ape.

"Quite dead," he announced. "It is too bad—he was a splendid creature," and then he turned to the work of liberating the Belgian.

He freed his hands first, and then commenced upon the knots at his ankles.

"I can do the rest," said the Belgian. "I have a small pocketknife which they overlooked when they searched me," and in this way he succeeded in ridding himself of the ape-man's attentions that he might find and open his little knife and cut the thong which fastened the pouch about Chulk's shoulder, and transfer it from his waist band to the breast of his shirt. Then he rose and approached Tarzan.

Once again had avarice claimed him. Forgotten were the good intentions which the confidence of Jane Clayton in his honor had awakened. What she had done, the little pouch had undone. How it had come upon the person of the great ape, Werper could not imagine, unless it had been that the anthropoid had witnessed his fight with Achmet Zek, seen the Arab with the pouch and taken it away from him; but that this pouch contained the jewels of Opar, Werper was positive, and that was all that interested him greatly.

"Now," said the ape-man, "keep your promise to me. Lead me to the spot where you last saw my wife."

It was slow work pushing through the jungle in the dead of night behind the slow-moving Belgian. The ape-man chafed at the delay, but the European could not swing through the trees as could his more agile and muscular companions, and so the speed of all was limited to that of the slowest.

The apes trailed out behind the two white men for a matter of a few miles; but presently their interest lagged, the foremost of them halted in a little glade and the others stopped at his side. There they sat peering from beneath their shaggy brows at the figures of the two men forging steadily ahead, until the latter disappeared in the leafy trail beyond the clearing. Then an ape sought a comfortable couch beneath a tree, and one by one the others followed his example, so that Werper and Tarzan continued their journey alone; nor was the latter either surprised or concerned.

The two had gone but a short distance beyond the glade where the apes had deserted them, when the roaring of distant lions fell upon their ears. The ape-man paid no attention to the familiar sounds until the crack of a rifle came faintly from the same direction, and when this was followed by the shrill neighing of horses, and an almost continuous fusillade of shots intermingled with increased and savage roaring of a large troop of lions, he became immediately concerned.

"Someone is having trouble over there," he said, turning toward Werper. "I'll have to go to them—they may be friends."

"Your wife might be among them," suggested the Belgian, for since he had again come into possession of the pouch he had become fearful and suspicious of the ape-man, and in his mind had constantly revolved many plans for eluding this giant Englishman, who was at once his savior and his captor.

At the suggestion Tarzan started as though struck with a whip.

"God!" he cried, "she might be, and the lions are attacking them—they are in the camp. I can tell from the screams of the horses—and there! that was the cry of a man in his death agonies. Stay here man—I will come back for you. I must go first to them," and swinging into a tree the lithe figure swung rapidly off into the night with the speed and silence of a disembodied spirit.

For a moment Werper stood where the ape-man had left him. Then a cunning smile crossed his lips. "Stay here?" he asked himself. "Stay here and wait until you return to find and take these jewels from me? Not I, my friend, not I," and turning abruptly eastward Albert Werper passed through the foliage of a hanging vine and out of the sight of his fellow-man—forever.

24

Home

AS TARZAN of the Apes hurtled through the trees the discordant sounds of the battle between the Abyssinians and the lions smote more and more distinctly upon his sensitive ears, redoubling his assurance that the plight of the human element of the conflict was critical indeed.

At last the glare of the camp fire shone plainly through the intervening trees, and a moment later the giant figure of the ape-man paused upon an overhanging bough to look down upon the bloody scene of carnage below.

His quick eye took in the whole scene with a single comprehending glance and stopped upon the figure of a woman standing facing a great lion across the carcass of a horse.

The carnivore was crouching to spring as Tarzan discovered the tragic tableau. Numa was almost beneath the branch upon which the ape-man stood, naked and unarmed. There was not even an instant's hesitation upon the part of the latter—it was as though he had not even paused in his swift progress through the trees, so lightning-like his survey and comprehension of the scene below him—so instantaneous his consequent action.

So hopeless had seemed her situation to her that Jane Clayton but stood in lethargic apathy awaiting the impact of the huge body that would hurl her to the ground—awaiting the momentary agony that cruel talons and grisly fangs may inflict before the coming of the merciful oblivion which would end her sorrow and her suffering.

What use to attempt escape? As well face the hideous end as to be dragged down from behind in futile flight. She did not even close her eyes to shut out the frightful aspect of that snarling face, and so it was that as she saw the lion preparing to charge she saw, too, a bronzed and mighty

figure leap from an overhanging tree at the instant that
Numa rose in his spring.

Wide went her eyes in wonder and incredulity, as she
beheld this seeming apparition risen from the dead. The lion
was forgotten—her own peril—everything save the wondrous
miracle of this strange recrudescence. With parted lips, with
palms tight pressed against her heaving bosom, the girl leaned
forward, large-eyed, enthralled by the vision of her dead mate.

She saw the sinewy form leap to the shoulder of the lion,
hurtling against the leaping beast like a huge, animate bat-
tering ram. She saw the carnivore brushed aside as he was
almost upon her, and in the instant she realized that no
insubstanceless wraith could thus turn the charge of a maddened lion with brute force greater than the brute's.

Tarzan, her Tarzan, lived! A cry of unspeakable gladness
broke from her lips, only to die in terror as she saw the utter
defenselessness of her mate, and realized that the lion had
recovered himself and was turning upon Tarzan in mad lust
for vengeance.

At the ape-man's feet lay the discarded rifle of the dead
Abyssinian whose mutilated corpse sprawled where Numa
had abandoned it. The quick glance which had swept the
ground for some weapon of defense discovered it, and as
the lion reared upon his hind legs to seize the rash man-
thing who had dared interpose its puny strength between
Numa and his prey, the heavy stock whirred through the
air and splintered upon the broad forehead.

Not as an ordinary mortal might strike a blow did Tarzan
of the Apes strike; but with the maddened frenzy of a wild
beast backed by the steel thews which his wild, arboreal
boyhood had bequeathed him. When the blow ended the
splintered stock was driven through the splintered skull into the
savage brain, and the heavy iron barrel was bent into a rude V.

In the instant that the lion sank, lifeless, to the ground,
Jane Clayton threw herself into the eager arms of her husband. For a brief instant he strained her dear form to his
breast, and then a glance about him awakened the ape-man
to the dangers which still surrounded them.

Upon every hand the lions were still leaping upon new
victims. Fear-maddened horses still menaced them with
their erratic bolting from one side of the enclosure to the
other. Bullets from the guns of the defenders who remained
alive but added to the perils of their situation.

To remain was to court death. Tarzan seized Jane Clayton
and lifted her to a broad shoulder. The blacks who had witnessed his advent looked on in amazement as they saw the
naked giant leap easily into the branches of the tree from

whence he had dropped so uncannily upon the scene, and vanish as he had come, bearing away their prisoner with him.

They were too well occupied in self-defense to attempt to halt him, nor could they have done so other than by the wasting of a precious bullet which might be needed the next instant to turn the charge of a savage foe.

And so, unmolested, Tarzan passed from the camp of the Abyssinians, from which the din of conflict followed him deep into the jungle until distance gradually obliterated it entirely.

Back to the spot where he had left Werper went the ape-man, joy in his heart now, where fear and sorrow had so recently reigned; and in his mind a determination to forgive the Belgian and aid him in making good his escape. But when he came to the place, Werper was gone, and though Tarzan called aloud many times he received no reply. Convinced that the man had purposely eluded him for reasons of his own, John Clayton felt that he was under no obligations to expose his wife to further danger and discomfort in the prosecution of a more thorough search for the missing Belgian.

"He has acknowledged his guilt by his flight, Jane," he said. "We will let him go to lie in the bed that he has made for himself."

Straight as homing pigeons, the two made their way toward the ruin and desolation that had once been the center of their happy lives, and which was soon to be restored by the willing black hands of laughing laborers, made happy again by the return of the master and mistress whom they had mourned as dead.

Past the village of Achmet Zek their way led them, and there they found but the charred remains of the palisade and the native huts, still smoking, as mute evidence of the wrath and vengeance of a powerful enemy.

"The Waziri," commented Tarzan with a grim smile.

"God bless them!" cried Jane Clayton.

"They cannot be far ahead of us," said Tarzan, "Basuli and the others. The gold is gone and the jewels of Opar, Jane; but we have each other and the Waziri—and we have love and loyalty and friendship. And what are gold and jewels to these?"

"If only poor Mugambi lived," she replied, "and those other brave fellows who sacrificed their lives in vain endeavor to protect me!"

In the silence of mingled joy and sorrow they passed along through the familiar jungle, and as the afternoon was waning there came faintly to the ears of the ape-man the murmuring cadence of distant voices.

"We are neating the Waziri, Jane," he said. "I can hear them ahead of us. They are going into camp for the night, I imagine."

A half hour later the two came upon a horde of ebon warriors which Basuli had collected for his war of vengeance upon the raiders. With them were the captured women of the tribe whom they had found in the village of Achmet Zek, and tall, even among the giant Waziri, loomed a familiar black form at the side of Basuli. It was Mugambi, whom Jane had thought dead amidst the charred ruins of the bungalow.

Ah, such a reunion! Long into the night the dancing and the singing and the laughter awoke the echoes of the somber wood. Again and again were the stories of their various adventures retold. Again and once again they fought their battles with savage beast and savage man, and dawn was already breaking when Basuli, for the fortieth time, narrated how he and a handful of his warriors had watched the battle for the golden ingots which the Abyssinians of Abdul Mourak had waged against the Arab raiders of Achmet Zek, and how, when the victors had ridden away they had sneaked out of the river reeds and stolen away with the precious ingots to hide them where no robber eye ever could discover them.

Pieced out from the fragments of their various experiences with the Belgian the truth concerning the malign activities of Albert Werper became apparent. Only Lady Greystoke found aught to praise in the conduct of the man, and it was difficult even for her to reconcile his many heinous acts with this one evidence of chivalry and honor.

"Deep in the soul of every man," said Tarzan, "must lurk the germ of righteousness. It was your own virtue, Jane, rather even than your helplessness which awakened for an instant the latent decency of this degraded man. In that one act he retrieved himself, and when he is called to face his Maker may it outweigh in the balance, all the sins he has committed."

And Jane Clayton breathed a fervent, "Amen!"

Months had passed. The labor of the Waziri and the gold of Opar had rebuilt and refurnished the wasted homestead of the Greystokes. Once more the simple life of the great African farm went on as it had before the coming of the Belgian and the Arab. Forgotten were the sorrows and dangers of yesterday.

For the first time in months Lord Greystoke felt that he might indulge in a holiday, and so a great hunt was organized that the faithful laborers might feast in celebration of the completion of their work.

In itself the hunt was a success, and ten days after its inauguration, a well-laden safari took up its return march toward the Waziri plain. Lord and Lady Greystoke with Basuli and Mugambi rode together at the head of the column, laughing and talking together in that easy familiarity which common interests and mutual respect breed between honest and intelligent men of any races.

Jane Clayton's horse shied suddenly at an object half hidden in the long grasses of an open space in the jungle. Tarzan's keen eyes sought quickly for an explanation of the animal's action.

"What have we here?" he cried, swinging from his saddle, and a moment later the four were grouped about a human skull and a little litter of whitened human bones.

Tarzan stooped and lifted a leathern pouch from the grisly relics of a man. The hard outlines of the contents brought an exclamation of surprise to his lips.

"The jewels of Opar!" he cried, holding the pouch aloft, "and," pointing to the bones at his feet, "all that remains of Werper, the Belgian."

Mugambi laughed. "Look within, Bwana," he cried, "and you will see what are the jewels of Opar—you will see what the Belgian gave his life for," and the black laughed aloud.

"Why do you laugh?" asked Tarzan.

"Because," replied Mugambi, "I filled the Belgian's pouch with river gravel before I escaped the camp of the Abyssinians whose prisoners we were. I left the Belgian only worthless stones, while I brought away with me the jewels he had stolen from you. That they were afterward stolen from me while I slept in the jungle is my shame and my disgrace; but at least the Belgian lost them—open his pouch and you will see."

Tarzan untied the thong which held the mouth of the leathern bag closed, and permitted the contents to trickle slowly forth into his open palm. Mugambi's eyes went wide at the sight, and the others uttered exclamations of surprise and incredulity, for from the rusty and weatherworn pouch ran a stream of brilliant, scintillating gems.

"The jewels of Opar!" cried Tarzan. "But how did Werper come by them again?"

None could answer, for both Chulk and Werper were dead, and no other knew.

"Poor devil!" said the ape-man, as he swung back into his saddle. "Even in death he has made restitution—let his sins lie with his bones."

ABOUT EDGAR RICE BURROUGHS

Edgar Rice Burroughs is one of the world's most popular authors. With no previous experience as an author, he wrote and sold his first novel—*A Princess of Mars*—in 1912. In the ensuing thirty-eight years until his death in 1950, Burroughs wrote 91 books and a host of short stories and articles. Although best known as the creator of the classic *Tarzan of the Apes* and *John Carter of Mars,* his restless imagination knew few bounds. Burroughs' prolific pen ranged from the American West to primitive Africa and on to romantic adventure on the moon, the planets, and even beyond the farthest star.

No one knows how many copies of ERB books have been published throughout the world. It is conservative to say, however, that of the translations into 32 known languages, including Braille, the number must run into the hundreds of millions. When one considers the additional world-wide following of the Tarzan newspaper feature, radio programs, comic magazines, motion pictures and television, Burroughs must have been known and loved by literally a thousand million or more.

Attesting to the unparalleled holding power Edgar Rice Burroughs maintains upon his readers are the many ERB fan clubs existing today. Established by dedicated Burroughs admirers, some of these groups publish their own fan magazines devoted exclusively to all facets of the Burroughs legend.

Interested admirers of Mr. Burroughs' literary works are cordially invited to write to the secretaries of these fan clubs for detailed information regarding membership and availability of their excellent Burroughs fan publications.

Readers in other parts of the world wishing to establish ERB fan clubs may write to Edgar Rice Burroughs, Inc., Tarzana, California, U.S.A., 91356, who will give every possible assistance.

Following are a few of the long-established fan groups:

The Burroughs Bibliophiles
6657 Locust St.
Kansas City, Missouri 64131

ERB-dom Magazine
Post Office Box 550
Evergreen, Colorado 80439

Erbania
8001 Fernview Lane
Tampa, Florida 33615

Jasoomian
Post Office Box 1305
Yuba City, California 95991